Dedicated to my wife Penelope,

and to the memory of my friend Alan Hunter.

The Colonial Boy

Geoffrey Storey

First Published in 2006

Published by
Paul Mould Publishing U.K.
15 Standish Grove - Boston - Lincolnshire - PE21 9EA

In association with
Empire Publishing Services U.S.A.

Library of Congress C-I-P data can be obtained from
the British Library, Boston Spa

ISBN 1-904959-46-6
U.S.A. ISBN 1-58690-047-1

Printed in Great Britain by
RPM Print & Design

Contents

Prelude

 The Soldier crouched by the door of the

Chopper, swinging the MG in an arc over the thick thorn-scrub below. The other three men in his stick were tensed to jump.

His adrenalin was pumping. Too many contacts. Too much fighting. Too much. He was exhausted yet felt on a high. Nothing was real, but this. The call.

The pilot shouted "Five minutes to contact." He stared out at the Bush. His Bush. The Bush he knew so well from boyhood. But now so unfriendly. Shite! Anywhere there could be a machine gun pointed right at him. Fuck. Concentrate!

He caught himself. His thoughts had drifted. He had heard snippets of conversation.

"Go for it!" said Gideon.

"I do love you," said Sue.

Sudden memories wandered in and out of his consciousness.

The way back home, the hot humid muggy heat could be wiped aside by a sudden thunder-storm, the air suddenly wiped clean, fresh and sweet, the smell of damp grass… the feel of home, the memories flickering in and out of his mind like still pictures…

The chopper swooped. The carpet of green became full of foci.

Individual trees. Individual snares, individual killers. He stared intently, looking for a sign. A clearing loomed up. The chopper hovered.

His Mother asking his Father to say grace before family meals in the old farmhouse out in the Bush.

The old mock-prayer, of begging, yet fatalistic at the same time, of Royal Naval sailors awaiting an enemy ship's broadside;

"Lord, for what we are about to receive, make us truly thankful…"

"Go, Go, GO!"

Chapter One

The Boy

The Boy sprawled over his bed. It was awfully hot. The tented folds of the mosquito netting sagged down towards him. Through his bedroom window, half-obscured by the frangipani leaves, he could see the full moon blotting out the stars. Sleep was not on tonight. Anyway it was the holidays. No need to do anything in particular first thing. Father would not be back for days yet. Mother only expected to see the Boy at brekker. No need to worry. No need to conjure up those images that helped sleep.

"Jude," he whispered.

Judy pricked up her ears, wagged her tail. She slept on the end of his bed, in her own little nest of rumpled sheet. The Boy's half-hearted attempts to sleep had told her that soon they would be going out prowling the night together. He reached down his hand and she silently licked it with a softly rasping tongue.

"Yebo," he softly said. She silently jumped down and went over to the water bowl in her corner of the room for a drink. Slithering out of bed, slipping his worn leather veldtskoene onto his feet and pulling on an old pair of khaki shorts took only a moment. Of course his old clasp-knife was always there, long and thin, worn by sharpening and use, looped on rope around his waist and tied like a gunfighter's pistol, and for exactly the same reason too. It was always with him and had as many uses as he had thoughts. One roughly hewn syllable named it, "I have Eaten," the cry of a young warrior who feels the pull of sinew as he withdraws his assegai.

But filling the pockets of his old bush-shirt required thought. There was a grubby handkerchief, matches, a torch, and a ball of twine ending in a hook tied in another cloth. He looked up on the wall, considered taking his .22 rifle. Of course. He'd never use it. That would wake somebody up. But the Bush was the Bush. Father had told him that always. He slung it over his shoulder, muzzle down. Bushman-style. There was no rain tonight. The air would be clear and crisp, carrying the slightest sound for miles. If he wanted the world, it was out there for him.

Carefully he raised the sash and cautiously looked up and down the wide verandah that ran around three sides of the house. All was quiet. The light of the full moon shone down from a cloudless sky, casting long shadows which might to another eye have concealed all manner of things. But not to the Boy. He knew his own back-yard. No movement among the outbuildings. Way out across the Bush the square windows of the Kayas were dark and empty. He knew Samson would be on guard somewhere but he was pretty sure that he'd see his fag quite a long way off. No. All he had to do was let the yard dogs know he was coming. He gave the soft cough of a feral dog. They would hear him and know it was him. They would probably not even stir.

He lifted one leg over the sill. Hoisted the rifle. Still poised to duck back in should he hear any movement, see any sign. Right. Go. Judy leaped out after him to stand on the bare boards of the high rafted verandah. This was the family's home during the hot humid summer months. Everyone seemed to have made their favourite place somewhere along its length. GranMa had her rocker near the front door, where she could see everything that went on anywhere that counted. From there she could shout right along the long corridor for Maria the cook, Elmira the little housemaid, or Philemon the house-boy. She had such a presence, had GranMa. She was so strict. So strict that every now and then he had to remember The Snake.

4

GranMa was from Home, a world far softer and far more pleasant than this land. She had only joined them when she had been promised - by an unenthusiastic Father - that "No, of course you won't see any nasty snakes. You'll be living with us in a nice normal home." Um.

Well, she hadn't seen any real snakes. Yet. Of course, there was the time they drove into Town to do some shopping and left the old lady quietly dozing in her old rocker, content with the world. They had quite a lot to do that day, and the Boy visited friends from school while Mother shopped and Father did some business. They all met up and ate in Father's club before going out as a family to see the sights. Grand fun. It was late when they returned. GranMa was still in her rocker, dead to the world, a contented smile on her weathered old face.

But above her dangled a snake's skin from the timber rafters of the verandah. Not just any old snake's skin; but a monster of a snake's skin. It must have taken ages for the snake to shed it, and she dozing unawares all the time. It was ginormous. All three of them looked at each other. They were all asking the same question.

It was Father who took over. "Right," he said. "The skin's right above her head. No getting that away without disturbing her."

"We have to get Ma inside without her seeing it?" said Mother.

"That's the idea," said Father.

Oh Boy. That WAS ten minutes he could remember all right. It was a very, very, private family joke now, but all he had to do if GranMa became too uppity was remember the snake. It was all the three of them had to do.

The household was really run by Philemon. Philemon was an immensely dignified figure, who ordered the household with an outward show of controlled ferocity. After all, everyone knew

5

he had been the heavyweight champion for the entire district in his time. There were quite a few betting men among Father's friends, who would still relish putting a few quid on Philemon either way. But the Boy thought he knew him. He was a good bloke and a great chum.

Off to one side was Father's favourite old wooden rocking chair, with his pipe-stand and big old mahogany ashtray. The boards there were scuffed and bore countless little match-burns. Mother was always trying to sneak a reed mat in under his feet but Father had this way of getting rid of it somehow in a way that nobody ever saw. And there was his table, when he was home it was piled high with books and magazines. His radio was in its leather case, tuned to the BBC no doubt. There was always some news about the war in Asia.

Tom was out there. Serving his queen and country. Oh, it was wonderful to get his letters. Always full of adventures and little anecdotes about the exotic east. The Boy had looked up every town that Tom had been to. Oh, what a life Tom was having. It sounded just like a perpetual big-game hunt, except the British Government was footing all his bills. And the game was unpredictable. Man-eaters. Armed with tooth and claw, but also with kalashnikovs. But it was their bush-skill against all those African boys, who had joined up after the party to beat all parties at the rugger club.

Those African youths had no doubt who would win in any contest. And now they were putting the insurgents to the test.

"Come on, Tom, what are you waiting for?" they had yelled across the bar. And with his lop-sided grin, Tom had moved over to join his peers as with whoops and yells they had driven into Town and woken up the recruiting officer. Blearily he had looked at their boyish, ruddy, fit, young faces, shining with sweat and with beer.

Oh, that made a great story, that did. That was his big brother, that was.

And Father listened every night to the news. The successes, the casualties, if any. Soon they'd have Television, they said. The Boy was really excited about that. But somehow, despite all that he had read, and knew, about TV, he still couldn't imagine such a flickering black and white screen out here in his home. Not really in the house on the hill. Still, there was Father's radio. Bringing him news from all over the world. The TV would serve the same purpose. And Father would get to see the match strokes too. Mad on cricket was Dad. He was always hoping to hear a good cricket score. Probably why he was the eternal optimist that he was, grinned the Boy to himself.

Meanwhile Mother had made her more gentile space just opposite Father's. When The Man was away all she had to do was swivel slightly in her chair and she had almost the entire valley spread below her.

The house stood high on a spur of the hill; smooth rounded rock jutting out over the veldt. Mother could gaze for miles over the endless grasslands spotted with isolated thorn clumps or baobab.

Or watch for movement in the quick little stream darting down the hillside beside her to be suddenly brought to a halt by the hot earth of the plain. After collecting itself in a little pool right at the rock's edge it began, much more slowly now, to move across her front to join a larger stream flowing down at the bottom of the slope, a sluggish river then, marked all along it's length by a fringe of more intense greenery and by trees.

Father's little dam on the river was as much to catch seasonal rainfall as to delay the river. The tall water-tank above the house and the bore-hole with its fitful wind-mill never allowed the family to forget that it was water that allowed them to survive out here in the parched Bush. Father's drilled waterholes dotted across the plain helped both stock and game to make it through the long dry.

But Mother rarely took much notice of the little river or the stream, or of the trees spotted across the plain, the denser patches of Bush, or of the gently moving dots that were cattle. Nor of the hazy purple mountains far away across the plain. The Bush was thicker there, fed by little streams that trickled down from the mountains but soon soaked away in the red soil. Father did not farm up close to the mountains. Far away were the rising plumes of smoke from kraals and villages. No. She was looking down the drive. Towards the Town about a day's horseback ride away in the old days.

She could observe almost the whole length of the drive, which left the main road from the Town about three miles distant. It was the bringer of excitement, of people, and of all sorts of things.

In the dry winter months a little spurt of dust was the first sign of a car or lorry turning off from the road onto the dirt drive. The Boy knew when to expect Father and would usually be high on the hillside, at the mouth of His Place, watching. By the time the Morris had moved up to the house in low gear he would already have scrambled and climbed and run down to the house. Letting himself in through the kitchen he would pass Maria the cook with a happy "He's here!" and rush through to the wash room. A quick dowse and flick, and a careful rush along the long corridor to his bedroom. There he would wait until Philemon announced the coming of The Man, the Lord, N'kosi, with a loud clanging of the old ship's bell, Birky, that hung beside the front door. He knew too that Philemon would wait till the last possible minute before ringing Birky, until he was quite sure that the Boy was ready and waiting.

It was the signal for Mother to appear, cool and collected as usual, and the Boy was expected to take her hand as they stood together on the verandah waiting, as The Man swung the Morris in a wide curve below them, angling the car for it's final climb up to the spur. Then Father's face would be frowning in concentration, as he placed the Morris just so and finally he would reach the flat open space beneath the verandah, climb out, straighten his rumpled Safari jacket, and look up at them.

His was a short pugnacious figure, broad and muscular for all his medium height, burnt a deep brown wherever the sun had managed to reach him - the Boy had seen him taking an impromptu shower under the garden standpipe after a long day's working in the fields, and had wondered at the contrast between the reddish pink of the rest of him compared to those bits exposed to countless days spent out in the African sun. His face was prematurely wrinkled by that same sun, his eyes squinting through the white glare. It made him look sterner and older than he was, because when he looked up at Mother and the Boy his whole face lit up and he grinned boyishly so very like the Boy's older brother Tom. He would shout their names, drop the briefcase that he had begun to haul over the passenger seat towards him, and bound up the stairs to them.

First he would hug Mother but soon he would grab the Boy's hand and whirl him round, asking as many excited questions as could the Boy. Then... but that was last time. And countless other times before that. Soon he would be Home again. Bounding up onto the long verandah like the best friend he was.

Father often took him out with him on his long train journeys around the country, even into neighboring colonies. The one thing that he remembered most was the little black picaninnies that flocked the dusty little stations, the big eyes and begging hands. Especially when the Bush around that station looked very dry. He never mentioned it to his Father. He believed Father would know how he felt anyway. The picture just became another part of himself.

The Boy had made his corner of the verandah right here, under his bedroom window, right at the back. The little stream wound down from the hill past his corner, and divided the garden from the homes of the blacks down on the more fertile soil of the plain across the river. He could keep an eye on most of the farm buildings, garages, and outhouses at the back too, as well as looking over the plain. The drive was around the corner, best seen from the front of the verandah.

The Boy still stood on the boards, listening, looking. Judy was delicately poised too; ears cocked, tail stiff. Finally she gave a very soft little whine.

"Yebo," he repeated, and stepped over the rail.

And tonight the moon was up. The game was on.

Down they crept through the moonlit garden to the plank-bridge over the stream that Phineas the carpenter had rebuilt only last year. Before that there were only stepping stones.

The Boy had asked Father if he might help in his school holidays and when Father had said yes it had been so very real. In his mind's eye he had been a Roman legionnaire laying the path for the legions to follow. Or his Grand-Dad, the engineer who led the first pioneers to this alien land, his eye always on the lookout for the slither of a greased body; the hiss of a thrown spear. Or the sudden stab of the assegai whose spirit was truly named "I have Eaten". Yes, Roman or bush warrior, the tricks were the same, the danger just as real and exciting.

He crossed the bridge. Suddenly a glow flickered brightly, and died back. Samson. The Boy dropped. He did not want to talk to grown-ups tonight. Tonight he wanted to be wherever the night was to take him, whatever the night was to make him.

Judy had dropped on her belly beside him, motionless. Here on this side of the bridge, across from the garden, there was scant cover. Bare rock with occasional patches of grass or bushes clinging on to life in crevices and cracks. He would not be getting his shirt or shorts dirty tonight, especially if he were to climb the hill up to His Place above the dam. He had spent most of the afternoon there alone with his books and his thoughts. At night the people of the farm could not bother him.

"Still," he murmured. Judy cocked her head, made no other movement. The burning tip of the cigarette swung away. He heard the scuffling of sandals growing fainter. Good. The last rounded bulge of the smooth rock was just ahead now. The two snaked their way to the sudden drop. To one side was the cut. Gigantic steps cut through it made their way downwards to the orange sand below. Smooth, worn stairs. Worn not by feet but by water, Dad had told him. Either the stream's old course, or cut by heavier rains, or the flashfloods of long ago, it led down to the dry donga. The donga did not meander across the plain like the river but sliced down through it like a sword-cut. Although it reached the bottom of the rock only a few hundred yards from the river, it cut away almost at right angles. It was the Boy's own highway, dark and secretive.

Deep and steep-sided, the sun's rays only reached down to the bottom at true noon - not the nonsense time told by watches and school-masters; but the real time of the sun. There the Boy could walk unseen by man or beast. There was simply nothing for any such there. Water ages ago had carried off any soft rock or soil. The wind kept it clear. Almost nothing grew. The stone was baking hot even now at night, in the wet summer of the long hols. The heat soaked into it. It was the way he knew the whole land had once been. Then had come the simplest little plants, then the tiny crawling things, and then - maybe just as the donga was being cut - his own ancestors, primitive ape-like creatures. But they had never mucked around with his donga. No. It cut straight on through the Bush, for miles and miles and miles. Right under the road, which was carried high above by an ugly concrete bridge. This was where the school-bus used to drop him off each afternoon when he was a junior at the Town school, before he was old enough to be a boarder in the City. It was only a little further to walk than being dropped off a few minutes earlier at the gates at the head of the drive. He had had to convince Mother and the driver that it was just as safe as walking up the drive- and a jolly sight cooler too.

Father had understood. He had walked it many times with the Boy and Judy. He had pointed out the layers of different rocks sliced through by the waters. He had told him the names of the few simple little plants that clung to the sides. He had known that as soon as the Boy returned Home he would ask permission to enter the study. There he would find Encyclopaedia Britannica, and the household would not see the little N'kosi, Nkosikani, for many hours.

Their feet had left no sign of their passing. The floor of the donga was bare. Hard impenetrable rock. Scoured. A few lizards scurried away from them, like miniature dinosaurs. The very ancientness of it all fed the Boy's imagination. And the quiet. Your thoughts could go anywhere in the donga. Alone in the darkness he could imagine far ahead of him the sound of marching feet echoing back through time.

Occasionally he was sure that they might just be carrying the lost Eagles of the Ninth up through a rocky Caledonian glen. He could smell the stink of sweat on leather, the weapon grease. But no, the best place to find those earthy cussing Italians was in a book, turning the pages alone in his High Place on the hillside, from where he could see for miles, and in his imagination see even further still, across the distant mountains away to the sea beyond and further to those distant islands far to the north which Father called Home.

These marching feet, so real to him, were probably a disciplined impi of the old King marching off to face the gatling guns of the Queen's redcoats, or the wounding fire of his Grandfather's irregular horse. But the feet were never of defeated warriors. Always, however doomed, he only heard the sound of men preparing themselves for glory. He heard catches of song on the wind, although he could never make out words or the language. It was the sound that thrilled him.

Walking the donga was not dangerous. Few animals came there. He could see and not be seen. Every so often he could clamber up the steep sides and peer over the edge at the world of man and of beast. Neither minded him much. They nearly all knew him, if they saw him at all. And anyway that was the last place they would expect danger. The days of outlawed men threatening a schoolboy were still far off. His world was what he made of it and what it made of him.

But tonight he was restless. Both the donga and the higher hills were places where he lived his own private day-time world. Not tonight. Tonight Judy made up his mind for him. Down below, amongst the Africans' homes, was a tough little something of a dog. Nobody minded Judy's doggy likes or dislikes since her visit to the vet, not even Mother. She whimpered and the Boy understood.

The little dog belonged to one of his earliest boyhood chums, Gideon. They had been inseparable, swimming naked together in the dam, throwing passes with an old rugger ball at each other, tackling with fierce disdain for injury on the iron-hard earth. Then, at about the time the Boy left to board in the City Gideon had graduated with his junior school certificate from the farm school Father was the patron of, and begun work on the farm in earnest. No longer in the holidays could the Boy go up to this man working in the fields and ask him to come out and play. Nobody told him this. He simply knew it was not the done thing. It would be a caddish thing to do. He and Gideon always nodded in passing, and talked at idle moments - but something had been lacking for a while. The Boy understood Judy however. For Gideon had a younger sister, Miriam. And to the Boy she was beautiful.

Not knowing exactly what he was going to do when he got there, he allowed Judy her head. Keeping a wary eye out for Samson (he wasn't a chain smoker after all) they moved down silently to the cluster of homes below them.

Each one was square and single-storied, white-washed brick with high ceilings to keep in the cool shade from the stoep that fronted them. Each was very similar, except for the headman's. It was larger and had a very imposing chimney. Father had worked to a plan, when he had built them. The carpenter and the animal-doctor had made theirs a bit posher by painting them a shocking pink and by picking out their window frames and doors in a brilliant white. Definitely not the original decoration envisaged by Father when he had replaced the old grass huts. There was the school-house. The old teacher, retired now from his job in the crowded bustling urban slums, lived there alone. He had been recommended to Father by a friend. For all his imagination, for all his love of the past, the Boy had never been able to see Father as a Feudal Lord. But perhaps that was why Father was The Man. The Boy knew all the houses in that dark cluster of buildings. He knew every family that lived in them; he knew some of their happiness and a little of their sadness. Just as they did his and that of his family.

What the Boy did not pick up through gossip and chatting he heard at the regular indaba between the people and Father. Then Father wore his stern serious face reserved for others. It was usually a low-key affair, in which matters which need not concern the authorities were raised and discussed. Only rarely were decisions reached. Slowly, gradually, as the people spoke, the opinions amongst the onlookers, the jury, would harden, Finally a sort of consensus would be reached, usually including even the wrongdoer. He, or she, would often propose his or her own punishment or compensation for the aggrieved.

Rarely did the headman or Father have much to say then. Their role was more to bring order and legitimacy to the proceedings. The Boy was often confused. Sometimes he would believe a man to be wholly in the right but when, ever so gradually, feeling against him grew, the Boy saw The Man suddenly crumble. From then on in The Man was lost. The Boy was brought up on a more combative literature. He often wanted to shout that this was not the way a Roman senator would behave, or an English gentleman for that matter. Ever since attending his first indaba he had become a devotee of the legal cases in the paper. This had nothing to do with the idea that every free-born Englishman was innocent until proven guilty. And bore scant regard for Roman dignitas either. But he had never spoken.

Especially after that one time many months ago, when a young man who had spent two years away down the mines had returned home with money to fund his bride-price, or lobola. He had done wrong. This proud young man had rejected the "judgement" of his peers, and had demanded justice in the white man's court in the Town. He had had his hearing, his day in court. And found himself leaving under armed guard to begin two year's hard labour.

The Boy had spoken to his policeman uncle about that recently but was laughingly referred to his Father, who in turn had said that he knew nothing more than the Boy had heard for himself. It was very difficult, this choosing between right and wrong. The ideas seemed very clear-cut. He had always understood and believed in them. He believed what Father and the schoolmasters had taught him; that the English common law was founded on ordinary decent common sense, as amended by Parliament to keep it abreast of changing times in a changing world.

The Boy knew that these people lived by destiny. His own people too, before their conversion to Christianity by Roman and Celtic missionaries, had believed in Wyrd, that invisible all-powerful force which guided everything. It lay behind the lightning in the sky and Thunor's thunder, but was unknowable, unseen, yet it ruled all things and all people. It gave life or death. It lay behind the epic poetry of the Old English. They had recited poems such as the 'Battle of Maldon' in the great halls of their people, and understood the tragedy that was about to unfold, as the brave heroes fought gallantly against the Norsemen, only to die to a man around their lord. That was Wyrd. Echoes remained in his culture still.

But here in Africa these people were not deciding by his law but by their own laws, which grew out of their own culture. It was a culture that he had grown up alongside and often lived by. His heart and his mind were at sixes and sevens. His friends were not his people and his people were not his friends, but he had few friends amongst THEM.

There was Gideon's house. And there was the window of the room which he shared with his brothers. The old signal? Yes. He picked up a pebble, threw it at Gideon's window. Counted ten, threw another. There was a hand behind the moonlit glass.

The Boy backed up beyond earshot. Waited. Judy sat still beside him, her ears cocked. Soon he saw dark movement behind the house. Silently he waited. The moving shadow parted unevenly, the dog going ahead and slightly to the left; the black boy following with almost exaggerated caution. They disappeared into a fold of ground. Then the two boys were together. The two dogs began their friendly ritual, noiselessly. Tails wagged. The two boys closed in the darkness. The game was on.

The Bushman

A greeting without words passed for the two boys. A nod. Then Gideon spoke. He had seen the rifle. "Eh, tomorrow is Saturday, so it is good that you come now. Tonight is a fine night for the hunt, a hunters' moon ."

Gideon only worked a short day Saturday, and Sunday was a day for the family.

"Down?" asked the Boy. But what he said was something quite different. Both boys spoke English and Gideon's tongue. And both boys mixed them up horribly, using whichever language seemed right just then. Actually, neither of them could ever be certain exactly which language he was speaking at any given time when they were together.

"Down," agreed Gideon.

They crawled even further back and along, both watching out for Samson or any other interfering grown-up. Then they began edging down, aiming for the great steps, which were the best way down to the plain below them. They moved silently, both at home in their world. School was a forgotten place to the Boy now. He was in his element.

Long after, at the very bottom of the hill, they stopped under a bushy tree thrusting alone out of the grasslands. It was unlikely that anyone could see them here from the height above but they were taking no chances. While they had been working their way down together it seemed that all the reserve twixt them had vanished. The old spontaneity returned.

"Right," said Gideon, "What now?"

"A touch-hunt?" asked the Boy. The most difficult hunt of all.

"Yebo," said Gideon. A "Yes" of eager anticipation

The two boys had not chosen the easy option. Even with his .22 the Boy could kill a klipspringer or a duiker at over 200 yards. Gideon, of course, reserved his assegai for warrior work but he could also throw his hunting spears phenomenal distances. The Boy had often joined in his exercises and was still astonished by how true those slender shafts could fly, and how lethal they were. No, they had not chosen the easy option. No way. They had set each other the most difficult and often dangerous work of all; trying to get as close as possible to some selected animal and then prove it by suddenly breaking cover and hitting it in any way they could with an ordinary light stick broken off the dry thorn scrub. Oh it usually never worked, in fact it never worked. But still, a chap could hope. And sometimes, when you had reached just about as close as you could, you felt that this time it was going to work, but of course those days seemed far gone now, but just the thought of trying for it again brought a surge of eager anticipation.

Other boys might have played games in the Bush. But not the Boy, or Gideon. They were young enough to imagine, to dream. It was on them, tonight, that the wagon-train, the kraal, depended for food. Both of them knew the Bush for the dangerous, even deadly, environment it was.

To step on a snake, still in the moonlight, not yet awakened by the warmth of the sun. Spiders, other carnivorous insects. Danger behind every bush, under every stone. And then the dangers the tourists he had met feared. The big cats. The wild dogs. So much less to worry about there, he told himself. But still, they were there. They would leave men alone if given the chance. He knew that. But Dad had told him that sometimes, without knowing it, you could really worry them. And if they felt cornered, almost any animal would attack. Instantly.

All those warning signs the tourists believed in from all their romantic novels were so much nonsense, Dad said. If you stood still to work them out you'd be dead, Dad said. No, just as the animals survived by instinct, so should you. Train yourself mentally, very much like the masters of Zen that he had read about high in his little cave. Every bushman, black or white, was a natural philosopher. Prepare yourself as best you can for every eventuality you could think of. And then when the moment came, as it would, then act.

Once he and Gideon had stalked an old Kudu cow, and got so close that they could see her udders swaying as she grazed. The Boy was entranced. This time he would count his coup. Geronimo! But just before he moved, Gideon had laid his hand on his arm. The Boy had subsided. Followed Gideon's lead and drew slowly back, deeper into the darkness, away from the moonlight. Then Gideon had pointed. Above where they had been standing was a gnarled old branch. And out on that limb was a shape. A lithe, sinewy shape. A poised Leopard. Other eyes had seen that old cow.

Gideon and he were friends. No word of thanks had been needed. Ever. Both their lives were as one. Either could have suffered from the other's mistake. Life and death. In the Bush. Where any moment could bring its own drama. Its own tableau.

No-one could really know how he would act in any given situation. But act you must. And it all came down to three options. Be still. Make no move. Retreat silently or fight with anything you had to hand. Gun, spear, stone, stick. Just as Tom might be doing now. No, don't think of Tom. That is a distraction. This is your Bush. This is your hunt. There were no chinks out here. This was no story, no romance. This was the hunt, your great game.

They moved on stealthily through the rustling grass. Fortunately it was not dry at this time of year. You could move more silently through the shoulder-high grass and the scrub.

From the hill on a baking afternoon it looked rather like a sea, this vast plain of grass, a sea with a few tree-tops waving, speaking of the island of shade below. In reality the grass grew in closely-bound clumps, strong and thick, with razor-sharp tips and edges, as incautious young uns soon found out. Sparse shoulder-high grass clumped around skeletal thorn trees. The moonlight was cut by the umbrellas of trees remote yet close in the moonlight. Something slithered. Another rustled. The empty Bush was yet alive.

A neighbourhood of competing life. And death. The Boy was no stranger to death. He knew it well. It's awfulness. Whenever he had been near death, whether of a wild kudu or a farmyard hen, he had seen only one thing. The light. The light in it's eyes. Extinguished. No more life. Before, long ago, they had also lived in a rented bungalow in the Town. There he had gone out with the other Town white boys and their guns into what they called "the Bush", the dusty rubbish-strewn outskirts of an African town. Under any shade-tree squatted a shanty with an old woman working, or old men whittling. Or staring into space. No roads. Not even packed. There was room. This was before the troubles. Before the great influx into the towns, and the new slums.

Beyond the shanties the boys cocked their guns and spread out. They began scanning the ground and quartering the sky for movement. One barked, rather like a gorilla. They all dropped. One or two would start worming forward. A gunshot would ring out. And there would be a mortally wounded creature writhing on the ground. Shock killed the pain perhaps, but not the fear of not being able to move in the face of it's predators.

The Boy usually moved forward then. He looked into it's eyes.

"I have not done this thing to you, N'kosi," he would whisper. Then he would fire. And the light went out of it's eyes. A vibrant living beast became dead meat.

The other boys had whooped, had run up shouting, had played push and shove. Then they had begun to wonder what to do. It was their quarry, yet it was often too big to carry home. And the idea of butchery was abhorrent to these little townies.

The Boy spoke. "It is good meat. I will ask Philemon to bring it to my house. WE will butcher it for you in the compound." And he had slipped away, sickened.

Oh, he would kill. If that was the only way. For life. Just as most of nature's creatures killed for life. And he would kill to protect his own. As would any of God's creation. But those days had taught him disgust. And in equal measure, Love. Gideon, a child of Africa, knew instinctively what had taken him many weeks to learn.

This was one reason why the Boy rarely sought out his own race. He too was a child of the Bush. His was not the world of traffic-lights, hooting motor-cars, and competing traders. That was Town life and he hated it and all it stood for.

In the City, however, there were libraries, museums, and parks, in which to ponder your dreams. Yes, the City.

But now, back in the real Bush, the two boys crept silently, always that relative thing. For silence in moving through the Bush was impossible. Slowly. Rifle cocked, short stabbing assegai hefted. for anything might loom out of the sudden darkness.

And then, suddenly, obscenely, those few miles away on what had been a still night, came the wailing cry. The Boy swung in its direction. There, high on its hill, above the living plain, was the house. And Suddenly all the lights were fighting the night, more flashing on as he looked. Fires sprang up in the compound of the workers. And the sound of wailing began to be joined by the shrill ulluliah of the women and the deep bass of the men's death song. A Chief had died.

Chapter Three

The Bushman and the Cave

 The Boy gestured at Gideon. Nobody would notice them now. "Run," his fingers said. A Chief has died. They ran, scrambled, back.

Silently they emerged on the shelf of rock, whereon the house stood. Light and sound, electric and piercing, rent the night. The boys stood poised. Without a word, just a nod, each broke away toward his own people. A Chief had died.

The night air was heavy. Slowly the Boy moved towards the house. Towards whatever awaited.

The rifle? He climbed the veranda, pushed that in through his bedroom window. Judy jumped inside too. But the Boy himself did not enter. He turned and walked towards the front door.

Philemon was there. He stood to attention, dropped his eyes. Philemon? Unusual. What ever had happened? Whoever had died? He moved along the corridor to his parents' suite. The door was open, and light streamed out. He went in. There was his Mother on the edge of the bed. Father stood close but off to one side. The light was that of the brilliant African moon, flooding in through the french doors. His Father's features were lit harshly by it. Every little line and wrinkle seemed to have become a deep furrow in cheek and brow. Perspiration bathed his face and was caught in those furrows. He had his hand on Mother's shoulder. That was not only perspiration on his brow. There were tears in his eyes. The Man crying.

The Boy saw it all. Ran into his Mother's arms. "Why all the fuss, Ma?" he gasped.

Ma held him close. Her voice was strange. "There's been bad news," she got out: "Tom..."

Father took over: "Tom is dead," he jerked. "A telegram has just arrived. Killed in action. With the regiment."

The Boy pushed out of his Mother's arms. He stood, mind a whirl. No. This had never been part of it all. Not Tom. Tom, the returning hero, Tom the chap who had won the hearts of all his chums' sisters. Tom the joker and Tom his friend. No, this didn't happen. Father had had his war. He and all the Boy's uncles had come back filled with tales of derring-do. You heard of people dying. But not Tom.

"NO," he yelled. "NO! Not my Tom!"

His Mother tried again to put her arms about him but he shook free. There was the light of tears in his eyes, a boy acting out an unknown play, and something else, new and never felt before. His Father did not even try to hold him. He looked at him before putting his arm on his shoulder: "He is with God, now." The Boy nodded. He was brought back into some kind of world of familiar ritual. It changed him. He felt stronger.

Tom his brother was a HERO. HIS Hero:

"Tom died for his King and for his country, didn't he, Father?" Words in a play. An ancient boy's magazine. Harry Wharton hearing of the death of a young subaltern in the Great War.

"Yes," said Father. Father moved closer to Mother. His friend. They each took the other's hands. The Boy saw, instinctively understood. Clenched his fists, moved from one foot to another.

He had to get out.

"Sorry, I must pray," he got out. Father moved to follow him.

"No," said Mother.

"He needs to be alone."

Judy quietly followed him out.

He gasped. Never had he climbed up to his little rocky ledge so fast. Like a young Greek athlete, the sweat seemed to clean him. He threw himself down at the mouth of his cave. The stark scrape of the bare rock was like a strigel on his naked limbs.

Here he was alone. Only Judy was welcome here. This was his home. His Place. His mind was racing, his heart beating, his head a whirl. This was not an escape. This was his reality. His mind dazed. His thoughts kept trying to return to what had been true so short a time ago. But they seemed unable to find their way back. Not now.

He pulled the bitch toward him. Hugged her close. Her soft tongue licked out. Finally the tears came. He knelt before the little altar he had built long ago. This was where he had talked informally to his God many times. On it were a few of his most precious things, above it an old pewter cross.

He began to pray.

"Our Father which art in Heaven,
Hallowed be Thy name,
Thy Kingdom come,
Thy will be done, in earth as it is in Heaven.
Give us this day our daily bread;
And forgive us our trespasses,
As we forgive those that trespass against us;
And lead us not into temptation,

But deliver us from evil.
For Thine is the kingdom,
The power, and the glory,
For ever and ever.
Amen"

He lifted his head.

"Lord, I Worship Thee. I Praise Thee.
As it was in the Beginning, is now, and ever shall be"

Ritual. Yet peace entered his soul. He was again within the parameters of his world. He stood and looked out over the plain. His world. He stood there a long while. Then sat, looking at the dawn. He went down to the house, Judy at his side.

It was quiet inside. Oh, the black people were there in the background. But they were silent. Whilst he was away Old Doc Macreigh had called. Mother was sleeping now. He passed the door to Father's study. He looked in. Father was seated at his desk, staring out of the window, gazing toward the mountains in the far distance beyond the plain. The Boy did not go in. He walked back to the kitchen. Gideon was there, waiting. The two boys walked out between the ranks of silent black people. They walked a long way.

The next day Mother's friends began arriving. Mrs. Smythe, the Police Superintendent's wife, the ladies from her club. The yard filled up with noisy children each with it's clucking nanny. Slowly the gears whirred. The pace of life in the house went up a notch. Everywhere there was talk of "Our Hero". Father took no part in this. He retired to his study after greeting his guests. That evening the Boy came across him at the bridge, smoking quietly.

"You are out late tonight," Father said.

"Yes, Father."

"You and I are much alike, son," said Father. He puffed for a moment. "Remember that Tom was not a hero for the reasons they give. He was your brother. He chose to do what he wished to do. Oh, he thought it right. As do I. He fought for the liberty of others in a far-away land.That made him a good man. What they say he did for his comrades, in the heat of action, that made him a better man than most. Be proud of him. Never forget."

"Listen to me. Tom freely volunteered to do the right thing. And he carried it through. One can celebrate the man in him. I believe that one day you might be told to fight. You will not be volunteering. Then, son, you will have to think for yourself. Remember this night. Remember your brother. Remember the chats we three have had long into the night. I believe that even now you know your own mind. Always try to do the right as you see it, son. And then see it through. The only Judges that count are yourself and your God."

In Town it was embarrassing. The way they looked at you, the brother of a hero. He tried to imitate Dad's politeness. He took Judy off into the park while Mother had tea with her friends.

The park was a miniature replica of Regents' Park in London, he supposed. Little quaintly-shaped lakes, pavilions and pagodas for the uniformed bands at weekends. The carefully manicured lawns and spreading shade trees. Away was a more tangled area with the outcrops and stones still standing. There he let Judy go and delighted in her wild joy careering around the Bush. But always he had to be wary. This was not Home. He watched her carefully, every few minutes whistling her back away from the traffic on the boundary road. Town-life was so constricting.

The funeral was unreal. An army guard of honour. Mother all dressed up. The ceremony the church did so well. The sympathy. Unreal. The Boy was in his tight suit. He slipped away, sat alone until it was all over.

On the drive back home he would share the back seat with

Philemon, watching the passing Bush slip by. River bridges with white water washing the rocks, the little pebble beaches, the Bush. Always the Bush. The further home he drove, the closer he was to Home.

After any outing to Town he would help Philemon unpack the boxes and bags from the car. Today, he knew that Dad was leaving again soon. There would be a braai tomorrow. Not just a barbecue, but a braai. Here the family were alone with each other.

Father loved the ceremonial of the braai almost as much as he did that of pipe-smoking. He built the log fire out in the brick barbecue carefully as Mother organised a party. First the framework of small branches, the bed of small logs, which would burn down to provide the charcoal. The tinder. The positioning. The testing of the wind. His tools; prongs and forks and long knives, water cup to douse the flames with a flick of the wrist. The preparation of the meats, the tried and tested marinades, the choicest steaks, lamb chops, chicken, and of course the boerewors. Thick, chunky, heavily spiced sausages (the Boy loved to tell genteel guests from Home, in an off-hand way, that the old settlers had so spiced their meat because they never knew when the hunters could next provide fresh meat for the achingly slow moving wagon-trains).

The little family unit was quiet that evening. Their public mourning was over. Each of them felt their grief, their loss, within. They knew it. They understood each other. It would be ridiculous to say that they would now be closer and stronger for it. No. They would simply understand each other better now for the way they had shared their grief. They were a family still.

They lingered around the fire long into the night, the coals glowing red and the air perfumed by the spices of their meal. Just outside the circle of dim red light lay Judy. She was perhaps the most content of them all.

Later, much later, Father had knocked out his pipe and said what he usually said, "Well, long day tomorrow."

With goodnights and hugs the little gathering broke up.

The Boy took Judy on her final walk of the day. He stood and stared up at the stars. The bright clear pinpoint stars unviolated by city lights. And he reached out. His mind tried to grasp them. The Romans and Greeks believed that a hero could be immortalized as a star. He chuckled for the first time. Tom was too modest for that lark. And anyway, he hated the heat... But out there was mystery, out there, beyond, he believed that there was the face of God. Out there was the best way for the Boy to imagine the presence of Him. All-embracing and yet his to reach out to. And this night he tried.

Father left early in the morning. Mother was left holding the heavy burden of guilt and relief among their friends and neighbors. A giddy whirl of parties, fetes, outsize barbecue parties prepared by black chefs in tall white hats, food being served by other black men wearing white gloves.

The Boy began to slip away from the house more and more. Quietly after brekker he would politely leave the table, mumble about having something to see to and then sidle out accompanied only by Judy.

They scrabbled up the rock to His Place, that forgotten cave high above the house from which he could see clear across the plain to the blue mountain haze in the distance.

In that confined hole in the rock his mind roamed free. None of his schoolboy friends knew of it. The household left it alone. Mother never intruded, not even with a question. Father knew. He had known of it long before the Boy. As with the donga he too had found the traces of the old ones, those older cave-people, and had told the Boy something of their story. How over the long ages the little yellow-brown folk had been pushed further

29

and further south, fighting bitterly, uncomprehendingly, all the way. The black conquerors, a proud race of warrior spearmen with their prized herds and fine material possessions, had not understood the little folk. Had neither wanted to nor cared to. It was a clash of cultures, which the Boy readily understood, but one perhaps so fundamental that it gave him an understanding of all those to come in his reading. Because the little folk were primeval communists. Their world a holistic one, the black man's possessions, his cattle, merely a convenient resource. So he ate the stray cattle and the outraged black men tracked and killed the little folk. And the little folk fought back ineffectually with his tiny poison arrows shot from toy-like bows. But they were so few, so scattered. They fought, ran, and died. Some survived in the deserts and mountains a little longer. And some still so survived. Others, like the children of the Sabine women, grew up amidst their fathers' destroyers. He saw many of their delicate brown features among the black men in the towns. But not among Gideon's people. They were princes among men. Warriors who had defied the gatling guns of the British.

Grandfather had fought for this land, he knew. Father had found it, much as he had done. But Pa had not been here since he had discovered it. That would not be the done thing. The Boy wondered sometimes if this place had been special to Father. He found scant trace of his passing however. What he did find were objects from long long ago. When he took them down to the house Father told him that some had been left by those little brown people. But some he could not recognise. Flints and rocks so formed that whether they be shaped by God or man he knew not. Perhaps from some early man-like being from so long ago that... The Boy dreamed.

He knew many caves. In these hills. In the mountains away over the plain. But here he found things he had never found in those other places. It might be that he knew every corner, had worked out the marks of long-dead hearths and middens, had spent so many hours examining the evidence, that part of him was that cave.

Evidence. Yes, here he felt like a detective. He lived among evidence. Of past lives, hopes, dreams. It gave him a sense of history, which he could not find in books. Not that he distinguished between book-learning and the history around him. It was all one. All fuel to feed his hungry imagination. He had been born into a world where there were honestly parts of the farm which had never been trodden by a white man's boot and hardly likely to have been visited by a black one either. His mind could soar as high as the eagles he could see above the mouth of his cave.

He could see far beyond the ledge at the mouth of his cave. Far away, all the way to that land whence his ancestors had come. Deep within the cave were chests filled with his discoveries. And with his books, his weapons. Everything he had been given, that he loved. All was there.

As was the photograph Tom had given him, taken in some army camp in Asia, surrounded by his mates. Men, who perhaps, for a while, knew him better than he did. But they would forget. He had lived with warriors all his life. He knew that but he would never forget and neither would Mother or Father. Their memories would be different but their own.

Memories. This place was where he lived through his imagination. He had few memories. He borrowed the memories from his books, from people he spoke to. The scenes might be of the past but the characters were firmly of the present. Tom had played his part. Homeric hero. Macedonian general. But now he saw his imaginings differently. Something hard and real had intruded. One of his actors had died. Nothing would be the same inside his head ever again. Now everything had shifted. Would always be shifting.

His boyhood images could no longer include the present. He could not think this, rather he felt something shifting. He would continue to see the world through the eyes of a questing boy, but would understand and interpret it as a man..

Tom had been more than a big brother. He had been his hero. Larger than life. He tried to imagine him dead. But it was impossible. He knew what a dead man looked like. He had seen a corpse down in the Kraal. When the light had left his eyes there was no more a man. He looked just like a dead animal. A sack. Just something shaped like a man. Now Tom was dead.

He retreated into the cave, beyond the daylight of reality. Deep within the recesses, where he had to crawl, were the old one's cave-paintings. The drawings still vivid, alive, the animals seemingly captured only momentarily by the rock. He had wondered long. Dreamt of a place conjured up so long ago by men so different outwardly, so alike in spirit.

Closer to the cave were his books. The Boy was catholic in his reading. Many were hand-me downs from Father, a lot more he had bought in Town, in the bookshops and scavenging among the shelves of his favourite second-hand bookshop. History predominated. But what was history? History carried the Boy into pre-history, so close to his own time and place, it carried him back to anthropology, sociology, politics, comparative religion, into geology, botany, and astronomy. He imagined building Stonehenge under the clear African sky. He searched for the planets. He wondered. At the Druids, at the mystical legends of King Arthur.

In a way it was his fiction, which brought him down from the dreams of long-ago. To characters who set bounds to his sense of right and wrong. He knew that they had existed for boys long before he was born and although they had been passed by in time back Home, out here in the Bush they still lived. Harry Wharton and the Famous Five at Greyfriars, their idiotic butt Bunter. This was still his world. Of boarding schools, fags, prefects, and schoolmasters to be respected, just and firm like Quelch, and young and athletic pupils full of boyish good humour themselves.

The Boy's world was a harsh one in which their values still had relevance. Life and death was real to an isolated bush farmer. As was the need to help others less fortunate than themselves. Charles Hamilton and Rudyard Kipling taught how to shoulder the white man's burden in their own ways, and their teachings still underlay the ethos within which the Boy lived his life.

In a few short days he would have to leave this, his real world, and go to school. There he could not escape into the Bush with Gideon or Judy.

It was real school. But perhaps not truly real. To a public school that was private and only for the exclusively rich. That meant for white boys, usually from similar backgrounds. Not all white boys went to such places. Most of the Town and City boys would go to neighbourhood state or grammar schools, places from which they went home every day and lived with their families.

He had tried telling Gideon all about these places. That hundreds of years ago they had been for the aspiring youngsters of England, places where those of moderate means could be taught by masters as educated as the private tutors who taught the young aristocracy. He had told him tales of the world that went on inside those quadrangles and cloisters... But Gideon had not been interested. A sort of shutter came down over his eyes. The Boy had found himself talking to... nobody.

Gideon's handsome face had darkened, "Why tell me of how things were, if now they are so different?" he demanded. "I enjoy hearing from you of the history of your people. As I know you love hearing of mine. But history has a purpose. It is not just... seman-tics. If that purpose has changed, you should not allow yourself to admire it any more."

"Now these places are not for the people. Even the rich of my people who go there become black Europeans. That is wrong. A man should learn about the world, about the customs of others, but he should remain true to his own culture."

He and Gideon were friends. They had rarely talked so between themselves. Some of his people might have regarded Gideon as a black Englishman. He knew himself to be an English African. And this dichotomy the Boy understood all too well.

His own culture, his values, were based on centuries, millennia of accretion. He knew he was not an African. Yet he knew that back Home he would not be fully regarded as an Englishman. He knew that but put it from his mind. In the present his world was in the past, a throwback to a time that perhaps had never existed. The vision he was taught at school was one that could only have been preserved in his divided society.

So, he went off to school. Judy he would miss most of all. At school only his imagination and his dreams would be his friends.

Chapter Four

City School

His days at boarding school were to be a dream, perhaps from his early days a nightmare, interspersed with solid episodes that he would sometimes recall later on. But not many. School was an atmosphere of unpredictable boys of all shapes and sizes, of steamy bath houses and blissful half-holidays, when he could escape into something more real than his own imagination. Such was the day he first met Sue.

After Dinner he had scudded down the oak-panelled corridor. Crikey. He would be late. The fellows would be waiting for him. He had lost count of the time that is all. And they would give him a hard time if they found out why.

His was the end study. The form passage was long, lined with studies on the one side, the other side formed by a high balustrade, polished by decades of young hands. He reached the end and half jumped, half ran, down the wide staircase leading to the hall below, bounding across the landings. A final clattering rush and he was almost at the open door leading to the quad.

"Blast!"

He did have this way of picking up a book to fill ten minutes and before he knew it almost an hour had passed.

And this had been no ordinary book but one he had asked Father especially to send to him. One by George Shion, a former Indian Army officer, who wrote historical novels in which the characters leapt out of the page. The Boy's imagination could really hear and see and touch and feel the exotic bygone worlds they inhabited. From Mycenaean Greece, where the men of Bronze battled their way through the uncertainties of their world in much the same way as the Boy felt himself struggling in a strange disjointed world of his own. Then the Roman Provincial Governor vainly struggling to apply logic and reason to chaotic Celtic Britain or the lone knight, an outcast from his own kind, who still fought to clear his name and his honour.

He ran. Clear of the stairs he put on speed for that final burst to the door. Almost at the bottom he heard a sudden roar of "BOY!"

He caught himself in mid-stride. "Boy," the voice boomed. "How dare you? You are a senior pupil in this House. You ought to be ashamed of yourself. Your actions are more those of a member of a junior form."

The Boy turned and apologised to the master. There was no point in giving excuses. He had behaved badly. He had forgotten himself. His apology was brusquely accepted and he continued on his way, more decorously. He left the House and crossed the quad towards the oak, where the fellows were to meet up before going down into Town by taxi to watch the visiting cricketers and then to have tea downtown. Everything seemed so quiet. No pupils were to be seen anywhere. The master's study windows were open wide, as though gasping for air in the sultry stillness of a half-holiday.

There was no sign of anyone when he reached the gnarled old tree. He looked around. Nobody. Then he heard a sigh, and heard Stephan say, "You took your time, old man!"

"Why didn't you go with the others?" the Boy asked.

"When you did not turn up I thought I'd wait for you."

"Thanks, chum." He punched his friend on the arm. "That was good of you, old chap," said the Boy. Stephan was an odd bird. Stocky, he still had a languid air, a deceptive appearance of laziness. He was, in his own way, rather an outsider. The son of a Jewish doctor he had never quite fitted in.

The fact that he was highly intelligent and continually scored top marks in practically any subject he took did not endear him much to the rather laddish fellows in the form. But at least he was not a swot, never seeming to have to push himself overmuch. And, like the Boy, he was rather good at games, even if neither ever made it into the First Eleven or even the First Fifteen for that matter. He was generous and helpful, so despite his Jewish background he was tolerated, rather than anything else, by the form.

The Boy and Stephan often found each other out, seemingly by accident. Kindred spirits. Oh, the Boy was popular enough by this time, stood his share of study teas and could certainly hold his own when it came to a fight. He had learnt more from the rough and tumble of the Kraal than any of the chaps, and he had had a lot of sparring-practice with his brother Tom. Yet he was quiet, somehow more in the background than the other fellows. He rarely stood out, never put himself forward. He was not shy but he did tend to steer clear of joining any particular clique or club. And there was always that slight element of "feeling apart". Perhaps he was still living the same dream life that he had in his cave. He enjoyed his books without being thought bookish. He managed to avoid being labelled. Such a one would be sniffed out by the chaps. There was nothing worse than being the odd man out at school. He had seen it happen so often. He trod warily, rather self-consciously, avoiding the inquisition of his peers.

There was another factor. Whatever your background the chaps soon seemed to merge into the school. The school had it's own ethos. Somehow this had never happened to the Boy but he tried to live outwardly by the rules. Even when they fell very far short of what he had expected.

Most of the other fellows were city-boys, whose fathers would not be out of place in any other big city. A few were, like him, the sons of ranchers.

The other chaps were good enough for the most part, but they took much for granted that he was uneasy with. Their casually calling blacks "munts". Their assumptions of superiority and acceptance of their place in the world was not deliberately elitist. It was simply how they said things. They had been brought up to take things for granted that even their peers back home would have recognized as "real". Unless perhaps one went back two or even three generations to before the First War. And hardly even then…

Oh, they had notions of honour-bright and fair play, and so much more. Those to whom such ideas applied though were definitely recognizable to them. Of course, some of the students were black. They came from both the wealthy middle-classes and from the old Tribal hierarchy. Long ago the settlers had learnt that the best way to control their new subjects was to absorb the old ruling elite into the new systems the white man had created. But they had gone beyond that.

Opportunities opened up in both the world of business and in such traditional paths to power as the church. His own form included the son of a Suffragen Bishop. The Boy thought little of it. They were a part of his life. He did not particularly think of them as different from him because of their colour. Rather because they were as much townies to him as most of the other fellows. He did not necessarily think of them as akin to his friend Gideon. They were certainly as far from being Gideon's sort as they were from being his.

The black scholars did keep a lot to themselves, in these so-called public schools that were so very private, so very elitist. Being a member of such a club created a new kind of border-line for them. As public school boys, they and their white fellows were separated out already from those in the state school sector. It was as if they knew that they were and were to be their society's elite. The blacks were fully part of the school, playing in both form and school sports and as varied in academic ability as their white counterparts. They used the same Latin tags and the same slang as anybody else.

One thing irked however. When they played games with all-white public or state schools the blacks were not allowed to play for the school.

The Boy had never liked team-sports. Life in the Bush had made him very fit and strong, but to tell the truth he had never liked any organized sport much. He saw no point in any of them. He would rather spend his time reading and walking. Fortunately both his headmaster and housemaster were pretty easy on the fellows in that regard and nobody was compelled to play.

Unfortunately the one game he did love he found himself hopeless at. Cricket. His Father had taught him the arcane jargon and traditional play as a very young boy. He and Gideon used to head up opposing sides. The farm boys all knew where silly mid on and silly mid off were stationed around the field. Deep point and deep gully was part of their everyday language. Everyone still chuckled though as a friend was told he was short leg.

He loved the individualism of the game, the ethos. A part of a team, you were an individual still. Batsman, bowler, fielder, all separated, each with their own game being played alone, in their heads and in actual isolation. Nobody could be as lonely as a batsman squaring up to the ball, with his entire team's hopes on his next stroke. Trying to read the sign in his opponent's eyes, mien. Holding and twisting willow in his hands. Waiting. Then the pent-up feeling releases as the leather leaves the bowler's hand. The bowler making his choices. The fielders, each a specialist in his own right, out there on the boundary, waiting, for something that might never happen but probably would with a moment's inattention. He watched his heroes in the sixth stride out. Watched the fellows from his own form. Played with them. Good enough for practice matches, for friendlies (not that many schoolboy matches were friendlies). But never good enough to be selected for a real match. An all-rounder, certainly. The only thing that he ever did that could be called good was at outfield. But nobody ever chose a fielder for a match.

He was to be poorly compensated in later life. Lined up with his fellow troopies, when a rugger squad was to be selected, the sergeant looked only at his size and strength and he was a "volunteer". There was only one team-game that he despised more. Soccer. So he counted his blessings.

The black boys felt their exclusion from teams selected to play for school against all-white teams. This became such a running sore that finally, and on principle, the rather liberal headmaster directed his sports masters to avoid such contests wherever possible. That was not that easy in reality, given leagues and championships. Fortunately many other schools began to agree and that particular recurring stab began to ease.

The white boys certainly felt superior. Not really as individuals, but as a caste. Not that they would ever overstep the mark even concerning a black boy and use obviously racist language. After all, these chaps were not ordinary munts. Heaven's sake, no. Open racism was not in good taste. Not when a black man had taken on the veneer of a white man. Give him a chance to prove himself. Otherwise that would be taking advantage and a fellow did not take advantage.

The Boy had found school strange at first. He had had a lot of learning to do - not scholastically, perhaps, but about his own peers.

After the tales of the Boys of Greyfriars and St. Jim's, schoolboy magazines from his own Father's schooldays, he had arrived thinking he would recognize so much in his new life. But he had not.

As a youngster he had hated the almost absolute lack of privacy, the steamy crowded lavatories and showers, the strict rules, the way each master and prefect interpreted them in his own way. A chap was always being caught on the hop. He tried his utmost to get away by himself whenever he could, steeling himself to go back and face them.

He said nothing of this to Mother and Father, of course. Anyway, Father already knew. He had been up to Magdalene. Father tired rapidly of the maudlin cracks he kept on hearing. Sometimes during the hols he and his son could play the anecdote game. But no complaints.

Oh, the public school he went to aped those of Home. They had similar traditions, uniforms, and buildings which were modeled on those far-from-public schools back Home. Spacious grounds filled with playing fields (there was always a "big side" for the seniors, and a "little side" for the juniors), with manicured lawns running up to the main college, traversed by a sweeping tree-lined drive. Along the boundary wall were wooded places where a chap could be alone. Even places where it was relatively easy to break bounds and clamber over into the free world. Oh, his school tried to be like it's contemporaries back Home. Yet over it the hot African sun blazed down from an azure sky. Scores of black gardeners kept its grounds spick and span, countless more worked inside. The boys were real-live African boys, not the clichés of his magazines. And the masters were much the same as he had known in day-school in his nearby Town.

The grub back Home could not be worse though. It was filling, he told Mother. Nuff said.

He was never to feel comfortable in the company of many people. He got on well with some individuals and a small number of like-minded souls. This enforced sharing of his space was to

41

stand him in good stead later though, even if it did force him more into his own mind, his own imagination, his own world, more and more. Not that he could ever escape the world outside his own. The other chaps might not have been turned on by politics, but long chats with Father had made him aware.

In Africa the master's study windows and that of the common room were usually wide open. Any junior could lurk close enough to a window on the hour to catch a snippet of news coming though on their radios. It was usually not very good. Later he could have his own wireless in his study. He kept up to date. Talking about what he heard, with anybody but a close chum, was bad form however.

The ethos of school was one he recognized of course. His schoolmates were inculcated with a way of thinking already way past its sell-by-date at Home. The ideals which had sent generations of public schoolboys out for two hundred years to rule a vast empire of millions with a real sense of self-sacrifice, and duty were still taken for granted. As the grandchildren of pioneers they still saw themselves as their successors, bringing English civilization to the benighted savage they were destined to rule, administer justice to, and to guide them to the point where they would be able to stand alongside their mentors and share in the bounty of their native land.

Still, he fitted in, in his own quiet way. Funnily enough as he moved steadily up through the forms he had more privacy in his life than he had had in day-school. And the boys were certainly a better lot than he might have expected of city-boys. He was neither popular nor unpopular. But the attitudes he was surrounded by made him feel apart. He had soon learnt just to shut up and say nought. What was the point? He was only a very small part of a great institution. He knew that for the most part remarks he heard all the time were not meant maliciously. Most of the form were hearty chaps and full of good cheer. Their minds filled with sport, competition, and not a little half-understood sex. There was little ill-will. They were just boys on their way to becoming young men. Even the licentiousness and sometimes downright viciousness of the real cads had it's own sort of boyhood innocence.

Stephan might have been a "Jewboy" in the privacy of a clique or when some boys chatted among themselves, but somehow even when said to his face, Stephan just took it in his stride. He never seemed to take offence. Just like the niggers and munts.

But Stephan was still an outsider. Oh, he was definitely a white man. And nobody in the school would admit to anti-Semitism, unless they were real bounders and cads. Bounders there certainly were in any boyish gathering, but Stephan never really found himself in an argument. His pater was a rather leftish opposition politician, but since at school nobody much worried at all about politics that was no problem.

"Well, what's up now then?" said Stephan.

"It's a half-holiday and I thought perhaps a stroll through the gardens, some tea, and then perhaps a taxi to see the end of today's play?"

"Sounds just the thing," grinned the Boy. "And with any luck we might add crumpet to the tea."

Truth to tell, it was deuced hot. And neither boy had on the khaki shorts they would have worn around the school House. Shorts were for young fags. They were senior men but their dignity cost them dear. Blazers and flannel trousers, topped with straw boaters. At least the gardens would be shady and cool, and they would only reach the match after the sun lost it's harshness and began to be a little more gentle.

Anyhow, what bird would look at a chap in short trousers, unless he was playing a game?

The two friends left the school by a side gate and stepped out onto the long avenue of leafy trees that led down to the Municipal Gardens. To each side as they left school bounds behind them the gardens broadened out, lush, exotic plants from the east mingled with rare African and European species. Paths wound their way through rockeries, miniature clearings, pools, and streams.

It was midday. There were few people about. A few housewives, the odd African municipal worker, a stroller or two, a pair of students from 'varsity college. Hand-in-hand they wandered off the main avenue towards somewhere quieter.

"Lucky blighter," grinned the Boy, as he admired the brown limbs and the long blonde hair of a girl as it swayed when her companion swung her off the path.

He knew darn well that if they did meet a couple of girls from the nearby young ladies' college they would be likely to find themselves sitting at opposite tables, perhaps sneaking a look or two at each other, but never daring to actually get up and walk over to their table.

"Shall we take a look at the zoo?" asked Stephan, as they passed the sign.

"Might as well," said the Boy, turning to follow the sign. They walked a hundred yards or so through the beautiful innermost heart of the parklands.

As they rounded the last corner before the aviary began they heard a shrill cry and just caught sight of a black man, dressed in the snazzy style of a gangster, pushing a lone white girl to her knees before grabbing her handbag and beginning to run straight towards them.

The Boy did not think. Before he knew what he was at he found himself carrying out a rugger tackle on the surprised gangster. They struggled for a moment but the man was too strong. He broke away, pushing Stephan to one side and bounded down the path, Stephan hot on his heels, shouting, "Stop, Thief!"

The Boy picked himself up, his mind on the girl. She was about his age, still sprawled on the gravel, her skirt way up above her knees, her hair disheveled.

"How are you, miss?" he asked, offering her a hand. "Are you injured?"

"No, I don't think so," she replied, taking his hand and using it to pull herself up.

"Here is your bag," he said.

"Oh, thank you so much," she said gratefully.

"Don't mench," he said, rather embarrassed. Her face was slightly grazed. He unthinkingly put his hand up to her cheek, "That looks jolly sore."

"Funny, I can't feel a thing," she said, ignoring his hand. "What about you? You hit that crook pretty hard."

She opened her bag and extracted a pocket mirror. "Golly, I must look a sight!" the girl exclaimed. He suddenly realized what he was doing and jerked his hand away.

"Oh, I'm alright," he said quickly. "And you certainly look okay to me!" He realised what he had said. "Oh, I didn't mean you can't be hurt. I just meant that you look okay…" his voice trailed off.

"I was a little grazed by the gravel," she said. "On my knee and cheek, but they don't look too bad. Look, not even bleeding!"

The Boy bobbed his head to look at the proffered knee. Hardly even any blood to be seen. But he knew that it was silly to take risks and took his handkerchief over to the fountain and returned with it. The girl bathed her cheek and wiped her knee clean.

"Promise you'll see the school matron?" he asked.

"Yes, fusspot," she laughed. He felt himself feeling very happy.

"Look, if you don't feel you need to get treatment for those scratches straight away, my friend and I were just going down to the café for a cup of tea or a coke. Would you care to join us?"

"Rather!" the girl replied. She looked a jolly person, her face cheerful despite the shock she must have had. The Boy remembered how he had first seen her, her legs almost completely exposed. He thought he had actually seen right up her dress and glimpsed her panties. Maybe more. He blushed, and the girl looked at him rather curiously.

"My name is Sue," she said, proffering a hand. He took it awkwardly, mumbling a rejoinder.

She was almost as tall as he was and wearing a light summer blouse and a thin, pleated skirt which seemed to swirl whenever she moved. She definitely was not plump. Just well filled out. Very well filled out. Her eyes caught his and she chuckled then grinned, almost boyishly.

Just at that moment Stephan came running back. "The Bugger got away," he shouted. On seeing the girl he caught himself, "Sorry, I meant to say that crook got away through the trees and I lost him."

"Don't be an ass," she replied. "But thanks, really!" The Boy introduced the two of them.

"Well, let's look on the bright side," Sue said. He got away, you captured his loot, and I'm not hurt. We don't have to go to all the bother of reporting this to the police, which will take hours off a lovely half-holiday!"

The boys heartily agreed and asked together, "So you are at school, too?"

"Yes," she said. "I'm from the north, and board at the girls' school just over the avenue from you."

"How come you are not in uniform?" they again asked almost together.

She laughed, "This is like talking to a chorus. Why don't we walk to the café and sit down. I feel a little whacked."

"Of course," the boys said.

Stephan added, after a moment, "Perhaps I'd better get along to the match."

The other two made half-heated noises, trying to dissuade him. Sue repeated her gratitude. He was adamant and walked off down a side path to the road to hail a taxi.

"What a nice boy," she said, as they watched him leave.

"Yes," said the Boy. He is my best chum.

She looked at him thoughtfully. "I thought so."

He did not know what to say. Nothing in his life had prepared him for this moment. Shyness began to almost overwhelm him. He felt his face coloring. But Sue took his hand and almost pulled him in the direction of the café.

Much later the Boy's mind was in a whirl. He found himself whistling that evening, as he walked back from the gates of Sue's school. She was the first girl he had ever spent so long with. Oh, he knew the facts of life – and had learnt them in the raw rough

47

and tumble of the Bush. His black play-fellows had not all been boys. And there had been Miriam.

He remembered what he had seen when she lay sprawled, her dress riding high. He would remember for a long time. His fantasies developed a new dimension. This was really different. And she looked and acted so grown-up.

It seemed that she often left school-bounds in ordinary clothes. Dress restrictions and rules for senior girls were a lot laxer than for schoolboys, apparently.

To the Boy it made her seem much more mature than any schoolgirl he knew. He did not really understand why she had spent so much time with him. She seemed out of his league. What luck. She really thought him full of pluck. And when he found himself mumbling that he had not really had time to think about what he'd done, she seemed to see even that as simply being modest.

Fortunately she did most of the talking. He found out all about her. Her home was only a day's drive from his. But so different the way she described it. Instead of dry thorn-bush and granite mountains, hers was a world of jungle and green ravines, rushing rivers and clinging creepers. Her people were farmers, not ranchers. She spent her holidays alone, like the Boy, with her parents. She felt the same oddness at school as he did. Finally he began to talk too. He found himself talking about everything; about the house on the hill, his friends there, and about school-life.

Tales of the Bush lead to his talking about both Gideon and Judy. Somehow there seemed little to say about Gideon to her. But about his old Judy he talked and talked. She had her own terrier, hers since a tiny tot, and they both happily swapped tales of their respective adventures. In fact their doggy tales completely broke the ice.

She had finally looked at her watch and said, "Oops! Better get back for tea!" And so he had stood up reluctantly, his shyness suddenly returning. He crossed over and pulled back her chair.

Together they walked back through the gardens towards her school. She repeated her promise to get her scratches seen to before tea.

"Righteo," the Boy said. He was feeling a little out of depth again.

"We must meet again soon," she said. As if she knew the Boy would never have had the nerve to say that first.

As they neared the gates she suddenly turned and gave him a thumping great kiss. "There," she said. "Now you know how grateful I am!"

And then she was gone and he found himself walking back in a daze.

He stopped in at the tuck-shop. He did not feel like having tea in the hall that evening. He needed to be alone. In his own study, with the door locked.

He plumped himself down in the study armchair and picked up a magazine. But his mind kept wandering. He began to remember everything that he could about her. What an ass she must think him to be so taken aback by that kiss.

He chuckled, remembering her cheeky grin, tanned but puckish face. No matter. Not with her.

Then he remembered her brown, rounded legs, her rounded thighs, her laughing face and her breasts as she leant forward on the table to make a point… Golly, what an ass he must have seemed to her.

But the memory of her femininity, of her natural open sexiness, began to dominate. He was glad that he had locked the study door…

That evening when he went down before supper he found all the talk was of the big match. He found Stephan in the corner of the common room.

"Enjoy the match?" he asked.

"Yes, rather," answered the other. "How did your tea and crumpet go?"

"Fine, I'll be meeting her again first chance I get," said the Boy rather proudly.

"Nuff said then," said Stephan, "are you coming down to supper?"

"Yes. Come on then," said the Boy, punching his friend on the arm.

Chapter Five

The Dam

Those Christmas hols, Mother had finally talked Father into taking her down to South Africa to stay with her family. The journey was many days by car. Father would have rather enjoyed the drive but Mother talked him into taking the train. The Boy was rather sorry about that.

Judy was an old girl now and he would have to leave her behind. Anyway, quarantine would have made taking the old dog impossible. This was going to be a real foreign holiday, not like last year at the dam. That had been a local holiday perhaps, but very different. They had all gone together.

Gideon had joined them the previous year, when they had rented a couple of rondavels near the peaceful lake below the great new dam. Father had told them how, years before, he had taken part in the huge operation to rescue as many animals as possible from the rising flood-waters. The government had hugely miscalculated that side of the job and volunteers had poured in to help as the call for volunteers had gone out.

Oh, the tales one heard from his uncle and the others were rather hard to believe. Such as the volunteers trying to land a bound croc on a flat barge, but good for a laugh nonetheless. The Boy had been little more than a child at the time so much of it went in one ear and out the other.

He did remember Gideon once asking why so few stories were

told about how all the original inhabitants of the green valley had been forcibly resettled. Or of the problems they had had in their new homes.

Then something had cropped up. He had not had to try to answer. Although in his mind he had already begun to frame words and phrases such as "new technologies, progress". Progress.

He sometimes thought of Gideon's musings though, when he came upon a starkly dead tree sticking up out of the mud, left behind with the high water mark.

Still viewing the great concrete arc of the dam at the mouth of the flooded valley was a real thrill. It was ginormous. They were able to walk along the top, looking in one direction at the river winding away through the gorge, and on the other side the spreading floodwaters. But that came later on a day's outing by car. The lake, where they reached it, looked like an inland sea. It WAS an inland sea. The blue water under the simmering azure sky stretched to the horizon. Everywhere near the shoreline were little islands, green and verdant. Life seemed everywhere.

Their camp was fronted by a small beach, on which they had their own boat drawn up. Along either side of the beach reeds and undergrowth grew right up to the water's edge. A well-tended lawn ran back to the rondavels, one for his parents and the smaller one for the two boys. The rondavels were quite different though they were circular with wattle and daub walls and thatched roofs with square glass windows in wooden frames. The doors were like the ones back home; in two halves, so that on a hot airless day only the bottom half need be closed.

Pa and Ma's bigger rondavel was roughly divided into three, a living room in which they sat and where they ate when not sitting around a fire outdoors, a kitchen attached, and a large bedroom - oh, and their washroom. The lavatory was shared by both huts and stood a fair ways away.

That of the lads was a lot more basic. A large room, furnished with a couple of cots, a table, and some chairs. Judy had her place on an old blanket by the end of the bed. She was quieter now, more middle-aged, less of a handful, and she slept a lot more, even in the middle of the day.

In their own rondavel they could imagine they were wherever they wished to be. Gideon entered into the spirit of his friend's imaginings. From planning a campaign in a general's headquarters to fighting a last-ditch battle against attacking tribesmen.

Gideon had taken up the Boy's love of re-living the past. He always had his own twists to the tales though. The heroic defenders of civilisation would often find themselves fighting to the end in a defiant last stand, with no rescue arriving until they had used their last bullet and broken their last blade.

Despite their warlike imaginings and evening re-enactments of long-ago, the scene was peaceful and the wildlife so different from the dry Bush near the farm. Butterflies and the birds especially. Hippos and crocs in the water and on the banks, water birds flocking on the lake, and fish teeming abundantly in the water.

There was still the cough of lion, the scamper of smaller creatures. In the morning there was often the sign of leopard prowling during the dark.

Gideon and he used to watch the animals, a veritable Noah's Ark, gather to drink in the early morning and at dusk. They did not even pretend to stalk them. Even their perpetual companion, Judy, lay doggo. That would have been too easy. But the lake itself was a different world for them.

The little rowing boat had come with the rondavels and Father had done his level best to teach them how to row a boat. Their lessons went slowly at first, almost seemed hopeless at times.

The two boys caught more crabs than anything, and all of them would end up in a sodden laughing heap in the boat with Father. After much splashing and shouting they had developed their own distinctive crawl. Judy would have nothing to do with this, no way.

But Mother was certainly not happy. She made sure Pa went and hired an outboard. That really set them free. Intended mainly for family outings, that outboard meant that the two boys, shirtless and in khaki shorts along with their battered bush hats, felt themselves fully qualified boatsmen. Damn it, even if the engine conked out, they could handle the oars. Use them as punts if need be.

Father let them out on the second day, one that was still and quiet. Father watched the weather closely before letting them go. Storms were notorious on this vast expanse of water. The thick rafts of weeds threatened at any time to stifle a propeller.

They took a long time to learn how to balance themselves on the flat-bottomed little craft, which was always threatening to throw either or both of the boys to the crocs. Finally however they had managed to synchronize things and to keep the boat heading on a more-or-less steady course.

They began exploring nearby islets, beaches, and bays in the lake. It was a vast expanse and Mother would not let them go too far. There were islands quite close though, and the boys felt like explorers as they nosed into the little coves and tied up to an overhanging bough. These islands had once been hill-tops, of course, and had been the last refuge of many large animals before Father and the other volunteers had managed to trap them and transport them to land. Now there would be few predators, only little unseen rustlings in the dense green. The islands were the homes of countless birds. They still had to watch out for crocs of course but crocs preferred to stay closer to the shore, where large game was easily come by.

The boys had heard the stories of crocodile dens. Holes in the bank into which the crocs dragged their prey. It was left to rot. Exactly as the crocs liked their meat. They had heard the tales of men and women, who had not been killed by the crocs and who had survived the journey under water to wake hours later in such a hell-hole.

It was hard to imagine. The boys had heard from Africans, who swore they had survived the experience through quick wits and courage. They had found, in pitch blackness, the route the croc itself used to enter and exit, and escaped. It made both boys wonder how many more had awoken in that hell and simply gone mad, or been too badly injured to try to escape, or feared meeting the croc coming home, or… they had given up on it. It was all too horrible and could only be coped with by making up stupid jokes...

Mother would often give them packed lunches to take with them. Then they would find a good campsite on the island and set about making a fire. Both of them could drink sweet tea by the pint in those hot humid lowlands. They used to try to avoid using matches to light the fire, practicing their bushcraft instead. Neither were scouts but their craft came from practice daily honed. They tried every fire-making method they had heard of or read about. It was a hobby with the two of them. They carried matches only as a precaution. Even when lighting just any old fire they would use their flint and knife-blades. They toyed with different rocks, with fire sticks, and experimented with new kinds of tinder.

They caught tiger fish. They were not good eaters but were real fighters. They would egg each other on.

"Come on, Come ON."

When the billy-can was gently bubbling and they were resting in the shade, they would talk. Of what they had done, of what they'd do. The Boy said nothing of Sue. Funny, he thought. This was the first time he felt no need to share something with Gideon.

There was something more. He felt somehow that it would be wrong to talk about her with his old chum.

He had met Sue as often as he could get away from the other fellows at school. That had not been easy. But as far as possible Stephan had helped him cover his tracks. He knew jolly well that she had had the same bother at her end. The longer they could keep things to themselves the better.

Sometimes he and Stephan would meet up with Sue or a friend in the park or in a café. They would take it from there. Go downtown for a movie. Or just sit and talk. They talked about everything. And they laughed a lot. They held hands sometimes. Sometimes she would give him a peck on the cheek. More like a handshake between two chaps, really, than a kiss.

Gideon and the Boy had often chased the same girls, of course, back home, and that afforded a few chuckles. Not abut Miriam of course. Those other girls had taught them a lot about life. By ancient custom boys and girls were very free in the kraal and could enjoy themselves and each other right up to the point of penetration. There was usually a rondavel set back where enamoured couples could entertain themselves. A girl had to be able to present her husband with her virginity. That was the only real taboo. It was all part of clan custom, a part of the rich tapestry of their life.

Making advances to a girl was one thing. It often worked the other way around, and the Boy was the one being chased. Then to find some privacy. That was where that isolated rondavel came in. There was no escaping in the Bush, where the real trial was trying to escape the attention of all those younger siblings.

The evenings were special on that lake. On a still calm night sometimes the sun would be a bright golden disc surrounded by an orange glow, creating beautiful colours on the rippling waters below. At other times the sun would be breaking through dark threatening clouds, and the whole world, not only the waters, would seem alien, so different from only an hour before. The shadows would come and go, twisting and turning the very trees under which they lay.

It was during the evenings, after they had eaten, that they would talk. Either when they were simply lazing in their hut, or mostly when they were lying by the fire yet apart from the adults in the party, the boys would talk about their plans.

The Boy was in his last year of school. He had no real idea of what he wanted to do. Oh, he would go south to 'varsity, that he knew. His folks could not afford to send him overseas for years. He would probably do an Arts degree, majoring in History or the Law. Something like that.

Gideon was much more focused. One night he leant forward and said, "I have been saving hard. Nearly all my pay. My family understand and will let me live with them for free. I study part-time. I am half-way to getting my senior school certificate. I have this idea. I am going to be a lawyer." He was determined to read law at the local university college.

The Boy was rather taken aback. He and Gideon shared many interests, history and law in all it's aspects being among them. But he had thought as little about Gideon's future as he had his own. To tell the truth, less. His first instinct was to feel rather hurt. How had his friend kept him from such a huge part of his life? How had he not known? There had never been any secrets between them before.

He caught himself. He remembered that he had said nothing about Sue to Gideon. Surely he had not expected his friend to be a manual labourer all his life? Of course not. It was merely that they had always been there for each other and he had not really thought of them being apart, pursuing separate careers. That was it, wasn't it?

That night they talked long and hard. About society and the rules by which each society governed itself. Tonight their conversation was more intense than ever before.

"It's hard to believe," said the Boy. "All these years your studying after work. We really have grown apart since I went to school, haven't we? I feel so lousy that I never knew. Never guessed. I thought that you were just reading as much as we have always done, working to…."

"Improve my general knowledge and my history?" Gideon grinned. "No, that's not enough any more. Not for a munt."

"No! That's just an expression. Like redneck for a Texan lout, or rock-spider for an Afrikaner. It is aimed at the type of person, not their race." protested the Boy.

"You cannot truly believe that. I have often been called a munt by those you'd call rednecks when I have been earning an extra bob or two working as an assistant at the filling-station." said Gideon. He was referring to the little garage about ten miles from home, which had a couple of petrol pumps and sold a few necessities to the white folk roundabout, and a lot of necessities to the blacks.

"Yes, but you cannot take their stupidity and racism to heart." the Boy began. Then he tailed off. Yes. He knew how he would feel. He had been called a Soutpiel whilst on holiday down south, and it had hurt. He did not have to take it too seriously. Boers were a resentful people, thrashed for their arrogance by men like his Grandfather.

Gideon's problem was that his people had also been conquered by his Grandfather and his comrades-in-arms. They were a defeated people. Never inferior. But defeated. He tried to say it.

"Gideon, our peoples were enemies once. They fought. Our

gatling guns and breech-loaders against your impis, assegais, and muzzle-loaders. Now our job is to learn to work together, to share this land. Remember, your ancestors took it from those who came before."

"Yes," agreed Gideon. "Forget that remark. I was not angry. Your people did win. And they brought us good things. We all live a little better for the big ranches, the railways, the police. And the law."

"Your law is our hope. We must make it our law. That is why I want to understand it. We have talked long. You have helped me to understand. How first it suited the English tribes to impose fines for murder, to have some impartial yardstick against which to measure murder, the value of men's lives. But then how in quieter times it became all about property."

"About both, Gideon. About safeguarding the lives and property of individuals in that society. And then about improving people's rights and safeguarding the distribution of wealth."

"No man has rights," said Gideon. "I could kill that man over there right now." Gideon pointed at a group of boatmen around a campfire a hundred yards away. "He has no right to life. Only that I and others grant him his life."

"That's it," said the Boy. "Society can only give its people rights, which it can afford. Everything else is just empty words. The English common law used to recognize that. There were no empty phrases about the right to life, liberty, or happiness. Right from the word go, in Magna Carta, there were simply specific rights and privileges due and owed."

Gideon nodded. "That is why we black people have to learn and to work, to make this land richer for all of us," he said. "That is why I must work hard to become a lawyer."

"Golly, it must have been tough studying late at night. It's a good thing Father gave the village their own generators just in time," the Boy said.

"Yes, your Father is a good man. A rare man."

"May I tell him about this chat of ours, Gideon? Tell him about your plans?"

"I did not tell you for help, I was simply sharing my life with a friend." Gideon said slowly, thoughtfully.

"Of course, I know that," said the Boy. "Come on, let's get this fire doused. I want to check out how these lake-people build their kraals."

"Without much style, I'll tell you that much," said Gideon. And was he right. The smell of rotting meat and human excrement almost turned the Boy's stomach as they made their way closer to the loosely-knit gathering of huts.

"Phew. I've had enough. I'm off. See you in the morning, chum." And he walked back briskly to the rondavel his parents shared. He wanted to catch Father alone, whilst he was alone on the porch, puffing on his last pipe before going in. He climbed the steps with Judy trotting at his side. Father was there, rocking back, puffing steadily, whilst gazing at the stars in the clear sky that arched overhead.

"Hello, son," he remarked, "What's the problem?"

"Problem? What, me? A Problem?" laughed the Boy. "Naw. No hassle. But I have just been talking to Gideon."

"Sound fellow, Gideon. I am glad the two of you are still such good friends," replied Father.

"Well, I've just learnt that while I was giving school a bash, he has been almost knocking himself out doing his senior certificate through a correspondence course," said the Boy.

"I know," said Father. "His father told me some time ago. He works shorter hours now, and the college sends me his bills," said Father.

"He never mentioned... I thought you did not know," muttered the Boy.

"Yes. I know. His father asked me to say nothing. He did not really think much would come of it. But you are right to bring it up. We should really help a bit more. He has a good head on his shoulders, and is a sound fellow," said Father. "Perhaps I can talk to somebody in Town. They might be able to put him up for a few terms each year with their boys. That way he will get his certificate much faster. Give him an allowance of course."

"That's great," said the Boy. "I'll go and tell him right now."

"I think you'll find he will be expecting you, son," smiled Father.

The Boy was rather thoughtful as he walked back to Gideon's rondavel, Judy at his side. He remembered Father's tales of the dam. Rising waters and the desperation of the animals. Graceful springbok or lumbering warthog. The way that they had fought for life, fought for life until the last moment, whatever and whoever they trampled on to breathe. Life is not fair, and selfishness is not ingratitude, but just IS...

Still, that holiday had been great fun. A real escape from the school, which had been getting him down lately.

This holiday, of course, Gideon could not join them. They would be traveling to Cape Town. They had holidayed there before, with GranMa, and the Boy had a fairly good idea how it would be for Gideon down south. They had apartheid down there.

Chapter Six

The Holiday

 The journey took weeks to plan. Mother gave up lots of her usual social pursuits and was, he was told, busily bustling around the house organising things. Fortunately they were due to pick the Boy up in the City, directly from school, so he managed to escape planning of the great trek, as Father called it. Father too had managed to ensure that he was very busy travelling over the past week or two.

When school broke up for the hols he met Father who drove him back to the hotel his parents were staying at. Mother was still busy with some last minute shopping so the two retired to the long verandah running right along the front of the hotel. A vast sweep of carefully manicured lawn swept down from the verandah to the gardens below. It was a beautiful evening, rather hot but the air crisp and clear. Very few people could be seen at the little tables that dotted the varnished floorboards. Even if they had been the space had been arranged to give maximum privacy. Businessmen and ranchers from up-country were often frequent guests and they expected no less. The ubiquitous black waiters in their crisp starched whites were everywhere but their presence was no more noticed than the fans overhead.

"Well," said Father, "less than a year now if all goes well. Then you will be going to 'varsity down south. This will be a good opportunity for us to have a look around."

"Do you still think I will be able to spend a few months overseas before I start 'varsity, Father?" the Boy asked.

"I hope so. So you had better get cracking and pass those exams, hear?" said Father.

"Sure thing," the Boy grinned.

"Hey, Father," he began hesitantly, "I have met a new friend. A real chum."

"Oh?" said Father. "Where does he live?"

"Well, it's not a 'he', Pa," the Boy stammered. He rushed on, "Her folks farm up north. They have asked me to come and stay with them for a couple of days before school starts again."

"Hmm. That sounds as if you are really friends, alright," grinned Father. "Righteo, old chap. We'll find a moment to tell Mother during this little trip. But I warn you, she is going to have a devil of a lot of questions for you."

"I know," said the Boy ruefully. Father was a good sport.

Next morning the taxi picked them up bright and early to take them to the station. They had plenty of time. The first-class sleeping compartments were slowly filling up, porters handing up some baggage, whilst most of the suitcases, bags, and boxes were destined for a van at the back of the train, just before the guard's carriage.

The platforms were wide and spotlessly clean, the people bustling around in an orderly but busy way. Off to the side was a row of little kiosks and doors opening into waiting rooms, cloakrooms, and station offices. The southbound was leaving from platform one. This was clearly the most important platform in the railway station. The other platforms looked quite like poor relations. Platform one sort of flowed out of the great concourse or hall of the station. The brightly painted metal girders arched overhead holding up the smoke-stained glass panels. The steam had created a kaleidoscope of colours in the glass. The Boy thought suddenly and irreverently of the City's Cathedral and its stained glass windows. Well, he thought, this is another center of worship in a way, isn't it?

While Mother organised the luggage and the sleeping compartment he wandered up front, to where the two locomotives steamed and hissed. Most of the time only one would be doing the work but he had heard that occasionally even a third would be needed to get the train over the passes. He found the engineers cheerful, helpful chaps and asked about it.

"Yes, that's right," they replied. "And it will probably be hitched on the end."

The smell of coal, of the fires in the boilers, the gleaming instruments of brass and copper, the levers and switches, all made for a magical world. But after only a few minutes chatting to the engineers a little black porter came running up to bring him down to earth. Mother wanted him in their compartment. He smiled at the engineers and strolled back down the train. Mother was looking really hassled, but he knew that she was enjoying this. Each compartment opened off a corridor that ran the length of the carriage. Their compartment was in actual fact two compartments joined by a connecting door. One was to be used by all three of them during the day and the other was to be his parents' sleeping compartment. The Boy would sleep on one of the couches that converted into bunk beds in the first compartment.

His first impression of the carriage was of thickly varnished wood with highly burnished brass and silver everywhere. Amply and comfortably upholstered leather made up the seats and the beds. He was told that their beds would be made up and their compartments cleaned out whilst they were at brekker in the morning.

Brekker. He was really feeling peckish. He should really have had more grub this morning. But the train was soon going to be moving off. He began stowing his hand luggage and put out what little he needed in the way of toiletries in the wash-room on the side opposite to his parents' compartment. He bounced around on the plush leather. Curiously folded down the little table that pulled down between the windows, covering the little wash basin that stood there. He toyed with the push taps, all in gleaming brass or copper, and then went to check out the lavatory. Hm. No surprises there.

Mother came hurrying in. "We should be leaving in a minute," she said.

"Where is Father?" he asked.

"He said something about finding out where the smoking car is," Mother replied. "You go along and have a look for him. That'll give me more space."

"Righteo, mater," he jokingly replied.

Just before he reached the lounge car, or smoking car, he heard the guard's whistle blow and heard the hurried slamming of doors, people shouting final farewells to friends and loved ones, and then the slow puff, puff of the engine. The carriages began to sound alive as the engine began slowly to move along the platform. He looked out of the window. They were well and truly off. He watched the station platform move slowly by, then they moved out through a maze of track with the City center sliding by. As the train began to pick up speed he watched the yards and factories slip away, the residential suburbs higher up the hillside. Now they were passing railway cottages and then the townships thronged the line. Small neat little boxes laid out along the roads, once white but now turned grey by the smoke of passing trains. Children waved and he found himself waving back, as he always did.

Finally the townships began to change into shanty-towns. Here the streets were not paved. Here the children did not wave. Then they too dropped behind and vanished into the early morning haze.

Turning, the Boy made his way to the smoking car, standing aside every few feet as adults moved around on their business. Fortunately he had not far to go. He enjoyed it, especially crossing over from one carriage to the other, the sky glinting through the connections.

Father was one of the few men in the carriage. The feel of the car was rich and sumptuous. Red leather seats around small rectangular tables, a small but well-stocked bar at one end, staffed by a cheerful looking black man in the obligatory white uniform. The bartender was talking quietly to the bar-waiter, a large muscular man with grizzled hair.

"What will you have to drink?" Father asked as he sat down beside him.

"Um, a Coke?" he wondered.

"No, it's eleven o'clock already. How about a beer?"

The Boy grinned. "Why not?" he said.

This was not the first time he had had a real drink with the folks. He had had wine at home with meals, when friends of his parents came round, but never before had the Old Man bought him a beer in public. He looked quizzically at the back of Pa's head.

His Father turned to the waiter but a sun-tanned burly Dutchman had got in first. "Hey, boy!" he called peremptorily. The grizzled waiter hastily made his way over to the last table in the carriage. "I'll have a whisky chaser, plenty of ice, okay, boy?" said the man. The waiter hurried back past them to the bar.

The boy and his father were quite near the bar, so Father stood up and spoke to the barman. "When you are finished, I'd like a couple of beers, please."

"Yes, sah!" snapped back the barman with a grin.

"As I was saying last night," said Father, "this holiday will be an opportunity for you to really look around and get your bearings down there. It has been a while since you have been there. You will find a lot of silly beggars like that chap down south. That's no way to talk to a grown man doing his job. If there is ever real trouble in this country, it will be because of attitudes such as his. I hope that you never get used to it but try to learn to live with them long enough to get a good degree." He thoughtfully lit his pipe. "But I daresay you will be finding a lot of pleasant ways of whiling away your time."

"I daresay, Father," chuckled the Boy. He sipped his beer. It was ice-cold. Brilliant. He looked out of the window at the passing lowlands.

The journey took days. Plains and deserts and mountains and simple cottages. Day after day. From jungle-covered hill country cut by ravines through which wild tumultuous rivers flowed, to snow-capped, lofty mountain ranges down to the harshest deserts that he had ever known.

Even the change of trains went smoothly. Mother never lost a thing.

On the final afternoon vast plains of grass stretched to the horizon.

Then only one more towering mountain range to cross before the peaceful serenity of a littler England, with soft pleasant fields, oak groves, rounded hills, as one crossed over the mountains to view the vista of the extreme tip of Africa. A beautiful fairy-tale peninsula bounded by two oceans and seemingly separated from

Africa by the mountains.

The exquisite architecture of the seventeenth century, scattered farmhouses and lovely little country towns. Vineyards and arable fields, woods and meres.

And in the distance the City from which European settlers first colonized Africa south of the Sahara. A European city in Africa. That was the essence of it all.

As the train made it's way down that glorious Peninsula towards the City, the Boy saw again the Europe from which those early emigrants had come. But more, much more. He saw in his mind a place far more beautiful, far greener. The day was cloudless, the sky a deep blue. Here there were no little black piccaninies waving at the train. They were a part of something much more sophisticated.

The train slowed, began to pass endless suburbs, industrial areas, and then their destination, the main railway station of Cape Town. It was not the buildings that seemed so strange. It was the absence of black people.

One only saw fair Europeans along with more swarthy Mediterranean types they called coloured. There were no blacks wandering the cobbled lanes, or on duty in the castle... the center of the City was at heart still a European city with it's great castle and lovely old buildings. But it was so alive. Right next to the station, as they drove by taxi up the slope to their hotel, was the bustling market-place, alive with colours and noise. A culture shock. The old buildings, the magnificent 17th century castle guarded by white soldiers, the veneer of Europe. But the people especially. White people. Coloured people who would be regarded as white, as civilised. No black faces. None.

As they wound up the narrow thoroughfares towards the hotel, the buildings changed slowly to Victorian public buildings and the views became more expansive the higher they went, all the way down to the harbour. The mountains to their front dominated all.

Finally they drove in through the pillared gates and along the drive to their hotel, what seemed to the Boy a gigantic Victorian mansion straight from the pages of Conan Doyle. They were greeted, arranged, and finally left in their suite with a marvelous view overlooking the City. The Boy rushed to the balcony. But Mother was there. Quite taken aback during the last few minutes by the efficiency of the hotel staff, she quickly set the Boy to sorting out his things. Father dutifully moved a few things and then headed down to the lounge "to find a paper and catch up with the news". The Boy had much more to do before he could make his escape.

That hotel lobby was to see the start of a whole new phase in his life. Oh, he had been down south before on holidays but now for the first time he was old enough to see things differently and not just to accept what he saw. Father was proved so right. The people were different. And there were in fact black faces in those crowds. Yet even between the coloureds and the white people themselves there were yawning gulfs, separation and deference, that he had never realised existed before. It was all part of a hideous social system that picked out every person and classified them, regulated their lives and dictated where they should work, live, be educated, and play.

Apartheid. A horrible word to hide something even more horrible behind. The Boy had grown up with the idea. It slowly began to become real to him.

As he watched social interplay in the bustling market or on the filling-station forecourt, the truth about his own life back home in the colony began to dawn on him.

Here the racism was overt. Expressed in signs on the beaches and on public notices "Whites Only". There were no such foreign signs at home. Oh no. They were too English for that. They played by the rule-book. Suddenly he thought of Gideon. At home were they not following those same rules? But simply more subtly in a more "English" way?

He worried that they were. And his head began to ache.

He had simply accepted that Gideon could not join him on this particular holiday. That was somehow wrong in itself. This place that they were in was all wrong. It made him think of things he had never really thought about. Certainly not on earlier visits. Then it was just a big European playground to him, with acceptance of what was. He was to learn how artificial this was. The segregated townships, the pass laws that determined where individuals were allowed to live, work, and go....

Crikey. Even lying on a beautiful beach with the breakers crashing on the sand in front of him he began to notice how unreal this seemed. Everybody on that beach was white. And tanning to become browner. He began to giggle.

"What's the joke?" asked Mother.

"Oh, nothing," he replied. And that sent him off into a real coughing fit of laughter. Oh cripes. This is so daft.

And it was to get dafter yet. The Peninsula was breathtakingly beautiful. All the people he saw seemed to be tiny insignificant actors playing their bit-parts against the backdrop of the most beautiful stage-scenery in the world.

The mountains, their lush forested slopes scarred by periodic fires. The quiet English tea-rooms set in manicured parks maintained by well-drilled black or coloured men in the background. The all-white suburbs with their all-white houses sending white children to white schools to grow up to work in all-white offices to finally retire to all-white clubs, all the time with an army of darker people working behind the scenes to support the whole blinking edifice.

Nice word that, he thought to himself. Edifice. Like Artifice. He began to laugh to himself again.

He laughed a lot that holiday. Everything began to seem faintly ridiculous.

But one thing was still true. This was by far the biggest and most varied place he had ever known.

It was a real family holiday. Father hired a car and they drove down through the City, snarled in traffic jams under the looming tablecloth of cloud covering the mountain. The air was fresh and clean, even in the Old City. The Old City was full of things to fire his imagination. Narrow cobbled streets, bookshops, toy-shops, balconies jutting out to almost meet over the street. The parks and gardens. The market in which people bought and sold almost every imaginable thing. Here the smells of east and west added to the colour and the noise. Down through the foreshore, with towering office blocks and modern skyscrapers, to the harbour. The ships. Royal Mail-steamers from Home, huge grey and white liners alongside majestic cargo steamers and grubby little coastal steamers. This was a new world to him. In few places was he to find the sea and land so intermingled, intertwined.

Fishing boats stole out from almost every little cove and port and launched from almost every beach along the Peninsula and late each afternoon the fishermen would sell in the streets or drive their fish-vans along through the suburbs, heralding their presence by blowing their traditional horns. And the beach was the place to swim, play, and relax.

Two oceans met here. Or a little way along the coast, as Father was rather fond of saying rather pedantically for him. The cold Atlantic breakers in the west and the warm shark-loving waters of the Indian Ocean in the east. Only a few hours apart one could enjoy two completely different oceans to play in.

Oh, a few years' time would see the Boy favour the fashionable rock-enclosed sands of the western beaches; bikinis and sun-kissed girls. But for now the warm eastern waters were for him - and for his parents. The brightly coloured little beach huts and fishermen with their nets. A day spent on the beach was anything but boring.

The Cape Peninsula was so diverse and beautiful. The cliff-top drives along the coast, much as he imagined the roads above the Bay of Naples to be, the little colourful fishing villages, the sandy coves at the foot of rocky cliffs, the large Nature Reserve filled with animals so familiar to him thousands of miles away to the north. But not the sea-mammals, the seals and perky penguins, the dour walruses. And here someone told him that there were more types of flora than anywhere else like it in the world. Oh, he believed it. He loved this place, he really did.

Further inland underneath the mountains that cut this Garden of Eden off from the rest of Africa were clustered beautiful little towns with whitewashed and gabled Dutch buildings dating back like those of Cape Town to the seventeenth century, as did the scattered farm complexes with their vineyards and majesty. Father rather enjoyed taking what he called the "Wine Route". The Boy thought it lovely too.

There was so much to do, so much to see, that the days just flew by. But then it ended. They drove down to the station next door to that old Dutch Castle, still a military headquarters, and boarded the train. Back in a compartment so like the one they had come down on, the Boy was content now to gaze out the window at the passing scenery and to remember. He knew that he loved that southern tip of Africa passionately. He wanted to go back. Yet he remembered all those seemingly ridiculous incidents that had made him laugh. Sometimes though he had realised that, ridiculous though they might be, they were not funny.

He had seen ordinary people treat other ordinary people, talking the same languages and wearing the same clothes, as not really people. He had seen people, whose lives were dependant on each other, ignore each other as if they had not really been real. And people far more similar in looks and language and culture than they had lived together and intermarried for centuries. It was different than between him and those friends of his on the farm. He knew that he was born in Africa. But he had never felt himself to be an African. These white people did.

And yet they ignored what was essentially African about themselves. He began to giggle again.

Heck, they hardly knew if they were calling their pet dog or their gardener.

The train rushed on.

Chapter Seven

Home

"**H**ey," shouted Stephan. He was staying with the Boy on the farm for a week. "You want to go into Town tonight, have a few beers?"

"Sure," said the Boy, as they trudged into the house. He slung his old bush-hat on the bed, ruffled Judy's ears. Judy had a very grey muzzle nowadays. She liked to take things more easily than before. But she was still a lively little bitch in her own way, he thought. He was not such a boy himself any more. Rather taller than Dad. Lean with strength in his shoulders.

Schooldays were behind them. That world was closed. After the ceremonies, the speechifying, Stephan had driven home with them. Mother and Father had come to the school for the graduation ceremonies, staying in their usual hotel. They had met Stephan's parents and had really taken to each other. Somehow it had seemed fitting that the two youths should spend a while together. Of course the Bush was not Stephan's world but he was fitting in well. Gideon and he somehow seemed to understand each other in a way that the Youth found rather ruffled his feathers. Somehow it made him feel the gradual widening of the divide between himself and Gideon more than ever. In a couple of days Gideon would leave for Town to complete his course whilst staying with a friend of Father's. He was studying hard and felt that he could not spend much time with either of the youths. His concentration was on succeeding in those blessed exams of his.

Oh, and his sister Miriam had married whilst the Youth was still grinding through his last term. That was that then.

He had not seen Sue for a while either. Probably would not for almost a year. She was taking a few months off touring Europe and the U.K. with her girlfriends. He was also going to England for a few months, but only in a month or two, and they had not been able to sort out any sort of rendezvous.

In fact he was feeling rather disgruntled.

This time at home seemed to be just a nothing time. A sort of interval between his longed-for trip to London and then his going on to 'varsity. The only sort of continuity in his life right now was Stephan. He would be joining him at 'varsity down south in Cape Town. Doing Medicine of all things. The Youth had as yet no clear idea what he was going to read. Oh, his parents tried to sit down and talk it through with him, but nothing had come of it. He realised that sending him off to study would be rather a costly burden on them. That he knew more as a kind of background thing, though. Neither had said as much to him. Mother had been the most straightforward about cost, saying that they "could not afford to waste thousands" if he could not make up his mind. Even this trip overseas was a luxury for his folks, he knew.

They had tacitly agreed to let the matter drop until his return from his trip however. Still, he found it hard to settle. He envied Stephan and Gideon their certainties. Even their acceptance of things. Dammit, things were beginning to be a bit of a hassle.

So a boy's night on the Town seemed just the ticket. Without Gideon his traditional expeditions into the Bush with a townie in tow held no attractions. He found it difficult to explain things that would suddenly grab his attention, intrigue him. To Stephan he was just looking at dirt. Getting hot and dusty and dirty with it. And he saw his friend's point of view at that. Just playing silly buggers.

That was all he felt he was doing right now anyhow.

Still, it would be only the second time he had driven the school graduation present he had found waiting for him in the drive on his return home. A gleaming yellow Ford Anglia, only a year or two old, polished by old Fred the garden boy until it shone. The Youth was certainly not mechanically minded. He knew how to check the tyres, oil, and water, and that was about it. He had learnt to drive on the farm years ago, as a real kid. This lovely new toy was the greatest present anyone had ever given him. He had rushed over to Mother and Father and hugged them both. Father's happiness was equal to his own but something in Mother's manner gave him pause.

Oh no, he thought. Not something else to feel guilty about.

He had taken it around the yard a few times and then proudly driven with Stephan to the petrol station cum garage cum mini-mart a few miles down the highway. Roaring back Stephan had had to hold on tight, shouting, "watch out for the cops, you silly blighter!"

When they turned off on the track leading back to the farm the dust cloud had risen so high and so thick that he had had to slow down. He could hardly see a thing. Despite his sheer happiness though he remembered the pain on poor old Fred's face at the sight of the car.

Damn. I can't go on feeling guilty all the time I have to have some fun, he said to himself. But the thought crept in, maybe not. You know that you won't be cleaning it again this afternoon, don't you?

And poor old Fred cleaned the car after lunch.

That car became one of the real loves of his life. He would clean it, Fred would clean it, he would polish it. But this was Africa. One afternoon he had promised to pick up Mother in Town. The clouds were glowering but he hoped the storm would just miss them. On the way back with her the heavens opened. Thunder rolled. The sky flickered with constant lightning. Hailstones the size of baby-fists began to hit the car. It seemed to him as if children were throwing rocks at his car. His car. He flinched as they struck, then gave it up as he strove to keep the car on the roads, driving slowly. His windscreen wipers could barely keep up. The sky was dark and menacing. The lightning itself was worrying. He had read about a car hit by a bolt. They finally made it back, along a dirt-road on which the dust had turned to mud with rivulets cutting across the surface and pools forming in every pothole. When they made it up to the house he squeezed into the car-port. There they sat, unable to leave the car. It was doubtful if even Philemon knew they were back. Even Mother was shaken and here they were in a car-port with a metal-roof magnifying every sound with big hailstones banging the metal over their heads and driving rain washing the woods and driveway.

When things finally settled down they bolted for the house. Well, he did. After helping Mother out of the car. Then, remembering himself, he stood on the verandah holding the door open for his Mother.

All night he thought about his car. Next morning he walked out early and looked at the damage. Dents and paint chips all over. Hell.

Father consoled him. Promised him to have her fixed up. Keep her garaged. One thing about taking her south, the weather was a lot more benign there. But oh damn. His car had had a right going over. He felt that she would never be quite the same again.

Father was as good as his word. After a few upset days the car was returned in an immaculate spick and span condition. Good old Pa. He had worked magic again.

Mother frowned when she heard the price-tag but the Youth did not notice overmuch.

So after dinner Stephan and his host climbed into the Youth's beloved car and roared off into Town. They pulled up at Mickey's, an Irish pub in the old station area. The place had an Emerald Isle theme to it, but in a very superficial sort-of-way, and few customers went beyond the usual chilled lager. The Youth had been there a couple of times with chums but in that small community had quickly become known to the landlord and his missus. Few girls came into the place alone but Mickey did have an eye for a good-looking barmaid.

This evening the place was very quiet. It was mid-week. The juke-box was on automatic and playing American Country and Western. Somehow after the day the Youth found this rather melancholic. Hell. Bellying up to the bar was not their style.

"Let's go get a table?" muttered the Youth. Stephan picked up his beer and followed. He was rather quiet, reading his friend's mood. He had rather hoped that coming out to a pub in his new car might take the other's mind off whatever it was that was bothering him. No such luck.

They sat down at a corner table. Stephan took out a pack of cigarettes and offered them. "What, and you the doctor?" said his somewhat surprised friend.

"Well, it's supposed to be part and parcel of the rights of passage thing, isn't it?" said Stephan. And don't tell me it's your first. You had rather a reputation for this sort of thing back at school."

"Oh, it's time for a few home truths now, is it?" grinned the Youth as he took one.

A couple of ranchers strolled in, greeted the two lads in the corner.

They ordered whisky chasers. Not Irish whiskey though, and not followed by Guinness either. They chatted quietly a while. Then the other two at the bar began discussing the forthcoming elections. Both began swearing about the British Government, bloody liberals, and uppity munts.

The two youths were onto their third or fourth beer by this time, and the Youth was beginning to chill out and to talk to his friend. The rather noisy discussion at the bar began to embarrass them both.

"Things are beginning to get heavy, though," said Stephan. "They are right about that. If the opposition get in, they are going to have a go at doing things their own way."

"But they are led by a bunch of racist Dutchmen," said the Youth. "Father seems pretty sure they have no chance of getting in."

"You can hear those chaps," said Stephan. "They seem pretty main-stream to me. That is the sort of talk I have been hearing for months in the City."

"But that sort of attitude doesn't seem to carry on over when they are actually dealing with blacks," said the Youth. "Want another?"

"Yes, thanks," said Stephan, rather owlishly, and giving the Youth a Nazi Salute. "My grandfather said the same thing in 1933, or something like it anyway. I do not like what is happening here, old chap. I really don't." He raised his glass.

"Hold on a mo," said the Youth. "These people are not Germans. They are as English as the day is long. That could not happen here."

"They are people, men and women, who feel threatened," said Stephan. "They want to hang onto the old certainties, and the world is changing. They feel that they dare not extend the franchise too far. The liberals and educated blacks want that. The British Government cannot go against what it sees as natural justice. So they will have to fight. They will lose but a lot of people will get hurt. And this country will never be the same again. I don't see much future here, chum, whatever the outcome of this election."

"What do you mean, old boy?" asked the Youth. "This is your country as well as mine."

"Perhaps," said Stephan, "but my people have more experience than most in simply trying to survive. I don't know though. All I meant was that perhaps when I have my degree I might think of looking for a job abroad. In the States, maybe. That is one thing about doing a medical degree. You find moving about a lot easier."

"I see," said the Youth. His mood was worsening again. He felt let down. His world seemed more fragile than ever.

He began to get angry. Not at Stephan. Not at his folks. At those bloody racists. He got up to buy another round, but Stephan said no, that they had had enough. Remember what he had said about survival? The Youth suddenly began to laugh.

The two got up and began to make their way outside to the car. "Mind yourselves," shouted Mickey.

"No problem," they called back.

The Youth fumbled for the key. Got in and revved hard before Stephan could fall into his seat. Stephan swung himself in, gasping. "That bloody door is sharp," he cried.

The Youth laughed, rolled down his window, took a fag from Stephan with his left hand, shoved in the cigarette lighter thingy (which he was very proud of – Father's car did not have one) and pushed his elbow out of the window. He drove rather sedately out of Town, remembering Stephan's warning and not wanting to seem more of an ass than he already felt.

But once he hit the straight highway out of Town he put his foot down. The road was straight in the blaze of his headlights, stretching seemingly endlessly for miles without a bend. "Always makes me think of the Romans and their roads, this," said the Youth, apropos of nothing, really.

"Yes, I know what you mean," said Stephan. Good to get some fresh air out here. Blow away the talk back there."

"I agree, old chum. Wholeheartedly." Turning on the radio he tuned into a pop-station. Or tried to. "Hey, fiddle with this thing will you? We didn't have time this arvy." Stephan jiggled the knob quite a bit before finding a station that came through loud and clear. The music was good too. The Stones.

"Hey, that suits my mood. Now all we need is a bird or two," yelled the Youth, driving faster. They reached the track leading up to the house. Suddenly he wanted to pee. Badly. He had never realized before just how far it was from the road. Blast. He could not take these potholes any faster. Oh well, at least there was no traffic here. He pulled over, shouted to Stephan, and began relieving himself off to one side. Stephan joined him and for what seemed a very long time the two friends stood side by side in the glare of the headlights, pissing and puffing on their cigarettes.

Both of them had rather sore heads in the morning. And not overmuch appetite for breakfast. Fortunately Mother had left early for some social "do" and Father had taken her in his car. The cook-boy was very amused at their condition though. He told Suzie the maid all about it. The whole household was chuckling at the Little Master. And the Youth knew it.

"Want to get out?" he asked Stephan.

"No, I think I'll just take it easy for a while," answered Stephan. He stood up and walked onto the verandah. The Youth grinned, feeling a little better. He asked the maid, quietly, if the paper had arrived. She brought it over from Father's study. The front-page was filled with strident political news and opinion. "Darn," he muttered to himself.

Just then Father came in with rather a grim expression on his face.

"What's up?" asked the two youths.

"I've just had my call-up from the Police Reserve," answered Father. "To cover the elections."

"I am sorry, Father," blurted the Youth. He knew his Father's views.

He was not the policeman sort of chap at all. No-way. But he felt very deeply about what he called his occasional duty to society. The Police Reserve was only called out in special emergencies, and both the Youth and his Father knew this was such a case.

Order had to be kept. It was not the rather genteel politics of the enfranchised classes that was the worry, but the threats of violent action by protesters from among the many disenfranchised.

Both he and his Father were angry that the outgoing government had done so little to broaden the franchise, claming that they had not the mandate to do so even in the face of both domestic and British pressure.

The concept of "One Man One Vote" had taken root in Africa.

"Yes," said the right-wing opposition. "But only once."

Father and son both feared the results of this election. They feared for the future of their society. For their country.

"Pa," said the son, "you have to, don't you?"

"Yes, son," replied his Father. "Somebody has to try to keep order, to try to keep us on a level keel."

"Damn," said the Youth. Hearing himself he fell silent. His Father grinned suddenly.

"Damnation is certainly where you and your friend are headed, if any of what I heard on my way in is to be believed." he said.

"That's the trouble with the set-up you have going here, Pa," the Boy laughed. "The grape-vine only reaches one way – to the top."

"I would call that rather selective criticism, son."

"Well, you did try to bring me up as a liberal, Pa!"

"And as one who understood the purpose of law and order, old man. They are in no way contradictions. Ideally we can hope that the outcome of this sorry mess is that we all realise the need to work together. Every man is entitled to his opinions – unless he tries to impose those opinions on society by force. This is still a tolerant society. But the forces of intolerance are growing stronger by the day."

"But if the protestors are denied legal expression at the polls, Father, is there any alternative to their turning to force?"

"There are always going to be cases like that," said Father. "But I do not believe that this country of ours has reached that point yet. There are enough reasonable people. We must be able to find a solution ourselves."

"Remember Tom," said Father. "He knew what he had to do. Even if it seemed to be in a moment of rugger-club enthusiasm. Somehow I don't think that you will ever need that sort of stimulation however. You are the thoughtful member of the family."

Two days later a subdued family stood on the verandah, the family place, with Stephan off to one side. The car was packed. Father was "answering the call". The evening before they had chatted, whilst Father cleaned his issue Webley revolver.

For good measure he took the old Mauser down from above the stone fire-place and cleaned that too.

Watching as he did so the Youth had felt unreal for a while. This was like something out of a John Wayne movie. The Indians were coming. Yet it was really happening. He felt a surge of affection, love, for his Father at that moment. He looked at Mother.

She looked as though she was holding back tears. She too was remembering Tom's farewell. This leave-taking would hopefully be for only a few weeks however. And Father would be coming home as often as possible. Possibly every week.

That was precisely what Father kept on repeating, as he climbed into the driver's seat. "Righteo. See you all soon. Remember, I'll try to phone as much as possible. Bye!"

Stephan put his arm on his friend's shoulder. "Want to take a walk?"

"I'd prefer a beer or two first," said the Youth.

The elections came and went. His Father had some tough dangerous protests to police. He never did find himself in a situation where the Mauser would have been useful. But he was a quieter man on his return. He had experienced the ugly violence of the City mobs, the discouraging talk of his fellow policemen, many of whom were fellow farmers and ranchers. He spoke even less after his return than he had been accustomed to before. The actual results filled the entire household with foreboding. The country seemed more divided than they had ever known it to be. The new Government called on all "civilised" men to support it. Although the franchise was based on certain non-racial criteria such as education and property qualifications, the fact was that nearly all white voters had the vote, and few blacks. That was a fact. Like most facts it could be argued both ways. By the right it was in no way similar to apartheid. Politically or socially. "Civilisation" could be aspired to by all, regardless of colour. Nothing except financial considerations or social distinctions common in most countries determined where one lived or socialised. On the left there was the clear fact that the majority of the people were being governed by a minority without any say in the system under which they lived.

No, it was not the doctrinaire apartheid of the south. Yet why should a man rule over another simply because his values were deemed superior? The word "civilised" was taken unquestionably as equivalent to westernised. It was not set in stone. Any man could become "civilised" through his own efforts or education.

It was so damned patronising when seen in that way. Everything he had imbibed as a boy went against that sort of thinking. He remembered Kipling's Gunga Din, even his Tommy Atkins. Both were patronised. Both better men than most of those reading their stories.

And remember to always factor in the British Government, answerable to another electorate, with it's own priorities, and answerable to world opinion.

His mood persisted. He was devoid of certainties. He and Stephan could feel involved in very little while Father was away. Or at least he could not. Questions were always there. His world had seemed normal.

He believed himself to be like any teenager in the western world. He and his friends liked the same music, watched the same films, wore the same clothes, read the same books.

Yet they were different. The past few months had brought that home to him. Their way of life, the only one he had known, was at the brink of a precipice. Articles in the papers, commentators on the news, were asking him to choose. Between two cultures. A western one and an African one. He felt unreal. He was not from Texas which seemed so similar in lifestyle. Wide-open spaces and barbecues. Nor was he from some Home Counties village with picturesque houses and a village green. Yet he felt even further from a country village in his own Bushveld a mere dozen miles from the nearest white family. He disregarded the lifestyle similarities to the America of the movies. Put what he believed were his values first. He felt that those values were more akin to that of a 'varsity man from Home than to a black farmer in the Bush. Was he likely to be more at home in an English pub than he was squatting in a kraal? Perhaps the fact that he would soon know the answer to that question added to his unease.

His small world was already becoming shared with other people. Not those from his books, whom he had invited in, but with journalists and columnists in all the media. The drums began to beat. Inside and outside of his head.

He was rather glad that Gideon was now away at college. He had left whilst Father was away on duty. The two youths had not had much to say to each other when the time came for Gideon to leave. Both thought that he knew the other's mind. Yet the white youth was surprised by the sudden intensity of emotion he had felt when the time came to say farewell. He had driven Gideon into Town in his car, with Gideon sitting in the back with his luggage. Stephan had stepped aside after saying, "Cheerio, then."

The two youths strolled on a while. The Youth had started saying "Take care, old friend..." Then he stopped. The two looked at each other. He could have sworn that he saw a tear in Gideon's eye.

He had anticipated this moment for a long time. He had left his boyhood treasures in the old cave. Why move them? There they had been important to him, there they belonged. In his past. He brought down from the hill a carefully wrapped object. The old pewter crucifix, before which he had had once knelt and prayed. The day Tom had died.

Gideon knew it. The tear swelled. Pulled a handkerchief from his pocket. A small copper good-luck charm given him by his Mother long ago. The other took it. He understood.

The two youths looked at each other. This really was farewell.

The Youth extended his hand.

"No," said Gideon. "The African Way." And he clasped the Youth by his forearm and his friend followed suit.

"The African Way!"

Neither youth added to that. Perhaps the thought flashed through both minds, "Does he mean what I mean?" Not now.

"Good luck with those damn exams," said the Youth.

"I'll do my best, old chap," said Gideon.

"See you soon, then. And keep in touch."

Of course.

Yet with Gideon away at college the Youth felt freer, somehow. He had space to sort out the questions that filled his mind. Stephan shared his doubts and some of the questions. Yet he had his own answers, his own certainties.

"I look at it differently, old boy," he said.

"There is not much that I can do to change things. I know what I believe is right and what is wrong but I am not likely to climb up onto a stage and shout those beliefs to an audience. And if a bloke cannot do that he is unlikely to change many people's minds. If I cannot do that peacefully then I am darned if I am going to stick around and become another person's political football. That is probably one reason I want to become a doctor. To help others without feeling that I have to fight for a cause."

All very well, thought the Youth. He knew that he disliked the thought of becoming a professional man like a doctor. For one thing he doubted that he had the ability. For another the idea of the job was simply too messy. Anyway, jobs like that required some degree of commitment, didn't they?

Dammit. The blazes with this.

"Stephan, lets ask some of the blokes around. They can stay over and if Mother agrees we can have a party."

Mother did agree. Arrangements were made to put the guests up. Clear across the Bush. She well understood that youngsters could hardly expect their friends to travel for up to a day for just an evening.

The phone-calls were made and that Friday arvy the blokes and the girls began to turn up. By car. By train. The little yellow Anglia began nosing it's own way to the station. A couple of neighbours on horseback. More for show and to impress the gals than for any other reason. Normally it was only rugger and cricket that drew these characters together. Both games had avid fans. The colony could field teams that could take on the best the world had to offer. As far as locals were concerned, however, they were not winter or summer games, just wet or dry. Both called for copious quantities of lager and lead to much camaraderie over the entire district. Probably such sporting festivals as there were, led to much of the community's sex and marriage games as well.

Rooms were shared out. A couple of empty huts in the Kraal served as outliers. Boys and girls carefully separated for now. At first there was tension in the air, wafted along with the winds of change., Too many boys were preparing for their call-up, others preparing to begin life as university students, well out of it. Choices had been made. And by girls as well as boys. Yet most of his friends were largely of like mind. Their choices differed but not their fundamental analysis. This was a chance for many of them to talk it out late into the evening and night. After all many of them would be together again soon at 'varsity or in the army.

But they were here for a party. Life juxtaposed. And life they had in plenty. They ate and drank. The speakers spoke in heavy metal. They drifted in and out of the house. They maintained a self-conscious awareness. All ate as they would have done if his parents were home or not. They left the hanky-panky for quiet corners. These were socially-aware kids. His Mother had known not to worry.

He and Stephan were the hosts. He danced, he played, he laughed and drank, missing Sue more than he realised. Then something in his mind clicked. He looked at them. Sun-brown and strong. Happy faces. Dressed in flares and skintight jeans, the clothes of four thousand miles away. He began to feel odd.

Late that first evening he sat on the steps of the verandah. There were signs of a storm and everyone had scurried inside. But somehow he felt out of it. His choices were not ones he wanted to share with any of those others. His choices were being made for him in his own mind.

The panorama that spread before him was one that was a part of him. He had observed it in all its moods but had never known it. This was Africa. The greatest, cruelest stage on earth. The thunderstorm broke far off across the plain over the mountains. The rain stayed away, but the brilliant pyrotechnics and the echoing blasts of thunder began to mute the sounds of the Bee

Gees from behind him.

The thunder began to quiet. The lightning quickened.

Then the rain came. He lifted his face to the cool, to the cleanliness. He felt strangely exalted. His soul seemed free. He heard the moving sound of Massachusetts, and his heart began to weep along with the emotion of the music. Then the driving hail drove him back under the verandah roof and the music seemed to blend in with his feelings, his thinking. The LP lasted for ever. His heart grew melancholic.

But the music changed. The voices of boys from far away caught up in another war, in choices so much like his own, intruded. Those 'Nam war protest songs hitting their mark, echoing those of those within. But the lonely, heady memories of the evocative sounds of The Bee Gees on the verandah that lonely night amidst a lightning storm staring down on his Africa beneath was going to be his memory, as long as he lived.

The thunderstorm had passed by morning. Now the air was fresh with the smell of damp grass. The party began to break up. Few had serious hangovers to worry them, few had done things they regretted. They had just had a good time. Today was for the open air and the Bush. They loaded their cars. Later on in the early afternoon the farm bus would ferry the train-travellers down to the station.

After brekker, boys raced their cars on the track and over the Bush with girls squealing beside them. They hunted and fished, scared the wits out of every living thing for miles around. Had a braai. Drank and shouted. He wondered. Joined in but escaped not. That party was theirs, not his.

The evening came back to him. The music. Not of Africa but of another world. He knew that he must know that other world; His world. He must know.

The twilight of an African summer's night closed in.

Chapter Eight

"What do they know of England who only England know?"

It was winter. The exit doors to the aeroplane opened. Hoo Boy, that cashmere coat he pulled down from the overhead luggage rack was just the ticket.

He stepped off the plane feeling more of a little boy than he ever had felt. Schooldays were behind him. An uncertain future lay ahead. He had been alone before but during the next few months he would really be on his own. Yet he was so excited. He walked through the airport concourse, looking for somewhere to catch a bus, pulling the cashmere's belt tighter around himself, protectively.

He had landed in Luxembourg, planning on taking the cheapest way to England and catching connecting coaches. It was perishingly cold, bringing a red glow to his cheeks. If anything it made him feel alive in a way that he had not felt before. Aware. He had wanted so much to see the magic white of snow but instead all was winter dull. Few leaves on the trees. Yet green grass everywhere. He found the bus-station. Nobody gave him the chance to finish a sentence in his schoolboy French, they simply all talked English.

He caught a bus to Brussels. He would always remember his first view of European houses. So different from what he had been used to in Africa. So many people lived in blocks of flats. The tiny balconies were alive with flowers and even mini-trees.

As they reached the outer suburbs he began to see chalet-type houses, neat and packed closely together, all in rows like chocolate boxes. Then the coach roared onto the motor-way, on the wrong side of the road. Man, he was going foreign for real now.

He saw little of the countryside. Who could from a seat in a coach on a motorway? He listened to his fellow-passengers for a while but little of their chit-chat was in English, so he began to doze fitfully. Soon the light began to fail and he found himself roaring on through the night on this weird journey, car headlights flashing towards him all on the wrong side of the road.

When the coach stopped in Brussels he grabbed his haversack and looked around. He had been told that there would be lots of cheap hotels nearby. He walked down the terraced streets. Terraces of houses, shops, and hotels, all intermingled. Like nothing he had known before. He walked into one hotel, asked at reception for the price of a room for the night. "What?" he shouted inside his head.

He had a timetable for the hovercraft crossings from Calais to Dover and hurriedly rearranged his mental timetable for sight-seeing. On his third try he gave up, and booked in at an outrageous price. Putting his stuff in a room he walked downstairs for his first European drink.

The price he was charged almost spoilt the lager for him. What the hell. The Eagle has landed. He bought another. It tasted just like a weak version of the lagers back home. He checked out the list. All lagers. It looked like he would have to wait for Dover to savour a real ale.

He felt in a hurry now. No, he would not do much sight-seeing here. He did not have enough money or the time. He would love to walk along the Apennines, visit Rome and Naples, see Vesuvius. One day he was going to have to check out the Greek mainland and islands. See the Peloponnesus, see for himself the diff between Ionic and Doric columns. But this was his folks' money. He knew he had no definite time limit. It would depend on what he could earn along the way. He could only do that in England. He did not yet realise that the whole of Europe spoke English. Although reluctantly, as in France. Even if he had, he wanted to get to London as quickly as he could. He walked across the street and ordered a burger. Same taste. So what? Back to his room. The coach to Calais was leaving early.

In Calais the atmosphere changed. Nobody finished his sentences for him. He struggled to be understood. The French were so touchy about their ruddy language that he was soon simply making his way by trying to follow the signs. He was told later that they had obviously taken him for an Englishman. He swore to wear his own flag on his back next time around. Again, he gave up on sight-seeing. His first experience of a French public toilet was going to be his last.

Salvation came at the hovercraft port. English and civilised lavatories.

He had just bought his ticket when he saw his first hovercraft thunder in from the sea and onto its concrete platform, the spray catching the sunlight. On board he was rather disappointed to find himself in a rather wide aeroplane seating arrangement far from any window. What the heck. He was almost there. He was almost Home, to the world that he had never really left in his mind.

At Dover it felt like his present and his past were coming together. The friendly offhand remarks in dialects he had heard only in fresh pink immigrants to Africa. Stepping out of the building the first thing he looked for was the first thing he saw. Dover Castle. It towered above him on the cliffs. His first real castle. He was really in England. This was his history.

Near here the Romans had landed to conquer these islands. From here the legions had left. He remembered that tale he had read and dreamed about of the last legionnaire turning back to light the beacon atop the lighthouse for one last time. His imagination began to people the castle again with figures from his history.

Hefting his haversack he trudged up to the castle. Despite the bare winter trees everything was so green. Looking absorbing. The white cliffs. The busy port below. He walked in. Far enough to see a bit, not far enough to have to pay the eager girl at her till. Just stood and stared. There was the surviving Roman lighthouse. Just as poignantly the early Saxon church. Or would it be Jutish? The Norman keep. The whole tale of defence and offence; the story of an island race. That brought him to thinking about the network of tunnels, from where the battle in and over France and the Channel Approaches was fought. Dunkirk to D Day. He looked at his watch. He had to go.

But Hey, this was going to be fun. He could handle this. The chicks down there in the streets looked cool. Everybody understood him. He knew where he was going. They used real money again. He knew which way to look out for oncoming cars. He was going to crack this.

Take the train to London? He'd see more, of that he was convinced after the past two days. No. He had better count his pennies, unless he could earn a bit extra over the next few months and buy an old jalopy.

He clambered aboard the coach, having given the driver his haversack to stow, and headed for a window seat at the back with legroom. He felt a veteran of coaches and busses now, He giggled at the urge to speak a bit of African to the white Englishman who was driving. Gad. Everything felt odd in this world he was in. A lot better than being on the continent though and even the chill air felt as if he had breathed it before. He could no longer see the castle. He was going to have to come back. But right now he had to get to London.

Unlike most of the other people on the coach he was not a tripper.

He had to get himself settled somewhat. Find a place to stay. Get inside of that still rather frightening place called London. Find a place his folks could write to, a place he could make a call from. That would lessen the feeling of being on the edge, help him to enjoy this new adventure. All the high blown justifications for why he was here spending his parents' money were really pretty low on the list of what he wanted to do. To grow? That meant little now. Now it was to crack it, to prove that he could do what so many young Antipodeans did. And do it alone on his own terms.

Hey these English chicks had long, cool legs and lovely hair. Pity about the faces and white pasty arms and legs but what the heck. The coach began to move. There were few people on board. No-one else had invaded his space. He did not stop to consider why. Not he with his long wavy hair down to his shoulders, lean, tough body and the mahogany tan of Africa. He was big and at a casual glance looked rough, enveloped in his overcoat.

He sprawled out, as it left the grey and red of Dover town. He marveled at the driver's ability to coax her around the narrow streets. And then the road to London stretched ahead. Dual carriageway. Not a quaint introduction to the Garden of England after all. He moved from side to side seeing what he wanted, an irritant to no-one. Kent was beautiful. More open than he had thought. But then the farmhouses nestling in their fields, the pretty village churches in the distance. He was certainly not going to see all he wanted to see today. He had changed his watch so many times already in the past few days but now, despite what it told him, dusk was beginning to come down.

In the evening dim the lights of farms, towns, and villages began to twinkle, giving the lie to the few buildings he had thought to see. By the crossing of the Medway (where the Romans once crossed on their way to battle the Britons, where English fleets for generations had been built, where the Dutch had swept the Thames clear of the Royal Navy and sent Pepys into such a tizzy, where...) the sky ahead was totally red with the illuminations of

London. London. A city still alive and working hard despite the night. Or because of it. He grinned and hugged his knees.

The coach turned off the motorway and began to thread through narrow two-way roads and then streets. He could see nothing much, merely get an impression of movement, bustle. He outlined his plans. Ask at the bus-station for a local paper. Look up the ads. Choose. Find his way to somewhere he could pay for a few nights' board and lodging whilst he looked for a place to settle. For a job.

Finally the coach pulled into the vast terminus at Victoria. He politely waited until he was the last to leave the coach. The crowds were pushing and shoving. He heard more languages in two minutes than he had ever heard in his whole life. He tried to help a lady with her bag. Was sent packing with a flea in his ear. Hoo Boy. No wonder the English keep themselves to themselves.

He looked around for a local newspaper stall. This was where prices became real for him again. He looked at the bewildering names and places. Turned to the section marked "Youth Hostels". A lot grouped around Paddington. He thought of the bear and chuckled. Right on. He followed the signs to the underground. The tube. The world's first. His first. He had studied the routes and lines on the coach ride from Dover, where he had bought a London map, an "A-Z". But at first the whole thing was bewildering. It was now rush-hour but to his surprise there was no pushing and shoving among the crowds. There was obviously an up side to the self-contained Londoner as well as a downside. On the train he saw how everyone seemed to have their space sorted out. Except him. With his haversack he took up too much of everybody's space and he was as relieved as his fellow passengers when he found himself pushing for the door at Paddington, muttering "excuse me, excuse me".

Then the problem he would find time and time again in the next few months in London. Getting his bearings. Working out which exit to take up to the surface. And when he got there, where the little area he stood in was in relation to his map. London was to become a succession of little islands around tube stations for him. Rarely connected. Complete little worlds in themselves.

He asked a busy looking attendant and crossed a busy road, walked down a side-street and stood on the pavement gazing down at a row of rather seedy hotels, which had probably been wealthy homes, surrounding a small railed-in square. A Church of England stood at the other end of the square.

Each terraced building seemed to proclaim itself either as a hotel or youth hostel. There seemed to be no difference. Each front door was reached by a short flight of steps. Well, if there was a lot of what looked like his sort of accommodation in one place, competition ought to keep down the prices. He soon found out it had not. Damn. No way he was going to share a room with three or four others and sleep in a bunk. He would just have to pay the going rate for a private cubicle and find work all the sooner.

And cubicle it was. But he had a window onto the square. A devil of a lot of stairs to walk up, and right down the middle of the building was a sort of lavatory/bathroom block with a door, a floor. The stairs wound around this curious smelly business. Right at the bottom in the basement was the breakfast space and around reception on the ground floor was a small lounge area.

Here he found himself among a real hotch-potch of characters from all over England and the rest of the world. He was willing to speak to anyone, pass the time of day, ask a question. He picked up gossip and survival hints. He learnt which local papers to buy. He walked back to the station, found a phone booth, telephoned home. Philemon answered. He left a message saying that he was safely in London and would phone back at the same time the next evening. He knew that Mother and Father would then be there. For now he was rather glad that they had not been. He knew that they would have returned the call and right at that moment he had not really much to say. He found a kiosk and bought a snack.

Then realised that he had had no need to. The pub which was his next stop had a full menu of English foods and light refreshment. And they mostly read like things his Mother would have made. Cottage pie, bangers and mash. He was back in the Motherland, O.K. He bought a pint of the dark brew straight from the tap. No lager this. And to heck with all the warm English beer jokes. This was just right for this piercing climate. He checked himself. Bracing. Yeah. Bracing. Certainly enough incentive to get his colonist Grandfather to set sail... But it was good. He had another. Listened to the buzz of conversation. Looked at the ornate mock-Victorian décor. This was unlike any bar he had ever been into. This looked more a way of life.

And hey, the clothes were the same. The hits were the same. This was his culture, man. He could adapt. This could be his style.

He walked back to the hostel, climbed to his little cubby-hole. This was quite a dump. He had better get out and about, earn some cash and find somewhere better as soon as he could. But that was on the morrow. He found himself gazing out onto the brightly lit square feeling sheer excitement.

In the next few days he found himself living and breathing through his imagination and his senses the sounds and sights of the seventies. Another version of "The Way Things Were". He had the long flowing hair, was taller than most Londoners and was deeply sun-tanned. He might have worn the same clothes but he still stood out from the crowd. Especially with his shyness, his politeness. He was here on a quest, but not as that sort of pilgrim.

He found his job as a personal assistant to a company director through a job agency. The first compliment he was paid by his new boss was how refined his English accent was. Hmmm. That was a back-handed compliment. With a start he realised how prickly the remark had made him.

The job made few demands on him. He only really spoke to his new boss. The pay kept him going. He stopped using his little hoard. He could finance a life now. Check out the scene. London was so big, so varied. He loved the place, the life, the history. He had few nasty surprises. He looked big. He looked tough. His accent could really pass as a toff's. He heard himself speaking sometimes, comparing himself to those around him. After a while his flatter vowels would out but not unless he relaxed. He was not an obvious target.

He spent much of his free time and weekends checking out the sights. Bloody hell! This was going to bankrupt him. A day at the Tower and Tower Bridge, followed by London Museum, that cost him half a day's pay. At least he could save a bob taking a decko at the Palace of Westminster and checking out the architectural landmarks. That was free. The National Army Museum and the Imperial War Museum got to him. Big. To turn into the Imperial and be faced by those mighty naval guns. That was the way to go.

He made his way by coach out into the "real" England to see an uncle and aunt. The view from the motorway was much as it had been in Kent. His destination was a single-story house, which the English called a "bungalow" in some awful industrial city in the Midlands with almost no history. They were good people. It was good to have close family here. It was good to talk about his Father as a boy. It was good talking about home.

It was hard to try to get them to understand his world though. All they knew was the rare television clip about some disaster or other. He tried explaining African distances to them. How that report had dealt with somewhere much further away from his folks than Belfast was to them. They could not see it. Their world was their "village" in their smoky city. Perhaps the county cricket team. It was there, with his own family, that he began to feel the stranger. He was keen to return to London. London, where he did not feel out of it.

When he took a boat down the Thames to Greenwich he felt really part of the scene. Up to now he had been closed in. London to him had been a series of islands around tube stations. He popped up into one, vanished again down a tunnel and bobbed up again somewhere else. The map in his head was not connected except in theory. But now he saw the broad panorama opening out for the first time. He saw the high chalk climbing in ridges on either side. The North Downs which were to push the Kentish promontory out into the sea curved closer to the south bank of the river here. One day he would travel down to the Medway and truly experience the sensation of the Thames Valley bounded by those great ridges. The buildings and ships along the waterfronts and embankments were the very stuff of his fertile imagination. The Tower and Traitor's Gate, as so many generations knew it. St. Paul's high above the skyline. The pattern was being stitched together.

At Greenwich he enjoyed the maritime history but it really did something for him when he climbed that little hill in the parkland behind and walked in the Observatory. The one point from which time and distance were measured. From here. He was there. In the centre of the world. Of his world.

London had one more greatness to offer him. The British Museum. Here he spent most of his time.

The history of the world seemed to be here. He became a regular in a few short weeks, on first name terms with more than a couple of assistants there. One or two he shared a beer with in the many and varied pubs of Bloomsbury. He absorbed so much in little time. His imagination was furnished with images, with pictures to last his lifetime.

Oh, he knew that London was England's magnet. That throughout its history it had swallowed up eager young migrants

102

into it's filthy disease-ridden maw. Until recently the death-rate in its verminous streets had outrun its own birth-rate. It had grown only by attracting the young, the fit, the adventurous. many of these were from abroad attracted to what was fast becoming the greatest city in Europe, but by far the greatest number came from its own hinterland, Britain, the City had always been dominated by the young and vibrant. Flavoured by the spice of the exotic. Right on. But that was not what he was looking for.

He answered an ad. for a room in a shared flat in Camden. His "landlord" was a rather prim and proper teacher, himself only a few months in London. His name was Raymond, a young teacher from Lincoln. He and Ray soon became fast friends and without too much hassle the Youth began to fall into a recognizable life-style.

He and Ray would often eat together in the evenings and then came their heading off to the pub. Ray introduced him to a few acquaintances. He was glad that he had not fallen into the southern hemisphere thing of clinging for support to other Africans, Australians, and New Zealanders. Having a braai or barby in common did not make for that much of an interesting conversation. Mostly they were just other townies anyway. Being born in Africa or Australia did not make them the bush folk they pretended to be. No ways.

Raymond himself spent a lot of time working and mugging up for his Open University degree, but many of the students he introduced him to were fun. His unorthodox background helped him to make up the couple of year's age difference between them and himself.

His work brought him into contact with a lot of people, some interesting. He was growing a little bit wary of his boss though, a bright young ex-Guards Officer who made him somewhat uneasy. Still, his first pay-cheque cheered him up. He was making more than he was spending. He threw himself into a round of pubs and bars, red wine, beer, and long talks into the night.

Then it happened. His boss had asked him out to lunch a few times. That had been a bonus. An invite to the theatre awakened his fears. What an idiot. The man was after his body. With all his upper class insouciance and manners, his guards' experience and good looks, he was suddenly, to the Youth, a degenerate. Somehow his time in London changed at that moment.

He waited until the last moment, so as to get another pay-cheque, being polite to the perv. and then he walked.

His acquaintances down the pub could not understand his feelings. He laughed at them and with them, and passed on. Even the girls in their sexy short clothing, appeared perverse.

He began to suffer mood-swings. Feel out of place. Most of these people were shit-ignorant. They know only their arseholes, because that's where they are at right here and now. Their self-deprecating innuendo, which still hide their patronising view of a world few tried to understand. The only England they know is an insular second-rate country. No Tommy Atkins? An 'elpful 'and? An Artful Dodger? They are too shit-stupid to wipe their own arses, no wonder they smell and are too selfish to pass the bog-roll round if they chance on it, so all their mates stink too.

He began to journey into his mind. Seeing his world where there is only their world. Damn it, a Kaffir has his culture to draw on, his God is a part of him, He is at one with the wholeness of the world, with his life. These Mother-fuckers are not aware of the side of the road they are on; their knowledge of science can't prevent them burning food, cocking up spices, or help them drive a car. Their televisions take over their minds, and politeness is food for humour.

You are not one of them. Degenerates. Their fathers were like mine... Perhaps. Your world is their world, if only they could see... no fucking schizophrenia for this Mother's son...

After a day's resignation there is still the pubs and gropes and freedom to revel in. Sue was too real for him though. Despite all the attention his good looks got him, he seemed shy with the girls. Swinging London. They were lovely, lively, intelligent. Compared to his Sue they were puddings. Dumpy little pasty puddings. The blokes were not much better either, he thought, looking around him.

But yet. He is from them. Perhaps they cannot see their world but it is there. He can see it. And not only in his mind's eye. The green fields, the haunting hills, the bleak moors of his ancestors.

Forget these fucking lower-class townies. Shit. They must be the same everywhere. He had them back home.

He began to burn to escape London. Blake's words came back to him. He was searching for his own promised land, his own Jerusalem. Not among these dark satanic mills, no, not there. He was looking for God's own country, where His feet in ancient times had walked upon England's pleasant pastures and mountains green.

"Or a Paradise lost," he chuckled to himself.

Right. Not quite. Not here in 70's London. London had only been his gateway. To search for the land of his Fathers. Of his dreams. The men who in their time had tried to build Jerusalem not only in England's green and pleasant land but throughout the Empire, throughout the world.

He had saved a bit. He bought a car. Another Anglia. More beaten up this time. Far less cared for. But he could work on it, if he could pay the taxes. He reckoned that he had enough dosh to last a couple of months, come spring. He registered with a temp. agency and began some odd-job clerking. Just enough to pay Ray's rent.

He began with local excursions, at first with acquaintances at weekends. The North Downs. The picturesque villages. The village green. The church. The pub. The ales. Then further afield one weekend. The South Downs to Kent, the Saxon shore forts, imagining.

He made that return trip to Dover Castle. Then on to Rye, returning to a night in Portsmouth, H.M.S. Warrior, Victory. The RN ships riding at anchor away in the distance. The evocative setting, over to Wight, the dreams crossing the Solent. The forest of The Weald.

His imagination stirred. He talked less to his "friends". He began again to live in his mind, his thoughts feeding his imagination. Then one day he packed in the temping, said farewell to Ray, stuffed all his meagre belongings in the boot and set off, skirting the cities.

He first drove south west, along that lovely coast-line. Shingle beaches below looming white cliffs. Many was the time he asked himself what he would do if he was caught on one of them with the tide coming in. He looked up for hand-holds, then chuckled to himself. He loved those little hidden caves, those stone arches shaped by the sea. Then there were those long sandy beaches backed by dunes, sweeping away into the distance. He loved the sea. Swore that one day he would live by it, near the sound of the restless waves. He loved the smell of seaweed, the calls of seagulls, its moods.

It was the picturesque little coastal villages that got to him most. The little harbours, rock-girt, and backed by the tiny stone fisherman's cottages. Each with their pubs and church. Sometimes a ruined castle on a headland. The boats drawn up inside the harbour here, pulled up onto the beach there. Painted bright blues and greens and reds. Lovely in themselves.

A drive to Stonehenge. The marvel of being able to drive almost right up to it. To walk around the stones. Feel them, if not physically then within himself. He was in a very special place. He looked around at the open empty land around about. He looked up at the tall aspiring stones and believed he understood what worship was all about after all. He would feel the same way at Cathedrals in Norwich and Lincoln. God was in all these places.

In all of them men had had a vision and that vision had carried across the generations. It had resulted in these cathedrals. And in this marvellous stone circle. This was glory to God. Not some cowering in a bare room but feeling the greatness of Him. He would see other stone circles, see isolated stones erected with tremendous effort, sit alone in small parish churches, their arches also raising the spirit up, ever up. Colour. Church towers. All built by men and women who proudly worshipped.

He walked back to the car, wondering. Time for a pint.

He hardly spent a penny except on his car. He slept rough at first, not knowing how long this adventure would last. Adventure it was. Through Hampshire, loving it's rolling hills, to Dorset, the chalk carvings on the hillsides and perhaps the most beautiful coastline he had yet seen. Lulworth Cove was his great discovery there. It was hard to find a place to leave his car, but he walked the coastal path for hours.

When he reached Devon he left the old Anglia in a village lane and walked onto Dartmoor. The day was overcast not wet. Somehow it made the experience better. He could not see the outer ring of tilled land and villages. This was it. An ancient world. He memorised his route carefully. He had heard tales of lost men on this moor. From hilltop to tor, counting and remembering each stream. Just like being back home but better. This was something else, man. He came across a ruined village, a mass of tumbled rock. He walked around, studied the discreet board and its legend, then finally sat down on a rock, just looking. He tried to understand how they had lived and worked from the traces they had left behind. This must have been a very different place once. All this seeming desolation, good emptiness, must have been created by these people and others like them. He knew the early Britons had lived on the high, drained ground. Clearing land for their farms had destroyed the light soils, allowed erosion, created bleak but beautiful moorland such as this.

He drove further west, crossed Bodmin, visited Tintagel and felt the atmosphere of the places. Finally he made it to Land's End. Or not quite. He saw the tourists, their coaches, and their predators, drove almost back to the beach at Sennen Cove and walked from there. He was certainly staying in shape. Both as a walker and a rock-scrambler.

Turning east through Exmoor he visited Bristol. He had to visit the maritime museums there, check out the City. After that, however, he left the hard south west and re-entered the softer green of Middle England.

He took the motorways on to the A1, the Great North Road, skirting the cities. This was the route traversed by those mysterious people we now know as Celts, the invading Romans, then the Anglo Saxons whose cultural descendant he was. William had come this way on his mission to ravage the north. It was the how travellers, mendicants, priests, and trades folk had travelled the land. His border reiver ancestors had driven their stolen kine along forgotten pathways parallel to the routes he now sped across, their hideouts known and their markets in East Anglia and Lincolnshire well-nurtured.

Now he had a pretty fair idea of where he was going and how long he would be. He had enough money. He booked into his first English country bed and breakfast. The landlady smiled a lot. The farmhouse room was cosy and simple.

He wrote to Sue, "Green is all. You know all about the wonderful history, the castles, the stone walls and the granite outcrops of the beautiful highlands, but down in the lowlands it is something much plainer which encapsulates England. The hedgerows of Merry England sum this place up. Nothing like it in Africa. We call neatly trimmed privet a hedge and bushes unlinked but standing in a row.

Here, a "hedge" can still divide large fields into the same areas covered by their mediaeval predecessors. They are home to lots of species of protected wildlife, and in a way remind me of the African Bush, of the life and death struggle we all face.

I have seen a rabbit flee from a Fox Terrier into it's crevice in the rocks of a hedge base. But a weasel had craftily positioned itself there to await bunny's return. One bite.

There was no way the dog could get at that weasel. However, nosing around the terrier pick up a stoat frozen into immobility by all the action going on around it.

The fields are so different, Sue, as you know. The blossoms are so bright and variegated, so beautiful. Some farmers simply grow flowers to sell. It makes for lovely patterns in the fields. You know that I don't know the names of all these plants up here, but I know what beautiful patterns are.

Hey, I haven't finished telling you about the hedgerows. Or about the stories I think that they tell. They can be free-standing trees or bushes, interlinked or interwoven. Experts can tell something of their age and even who grew them just by studying them. I chatted to a bloke on the Downs once. I think I can work out the age of the one bordering the footpath behind us. I get a bit mixed up, I admit. But I think it goes something like this. It might go back at least to the late Neolithic/Late Bronze Age, from it's ditch and embankment; the absence of stonework. Along with its lack of the trees being intertwined. That's an Iron Age/Old English fashion. Oh, I don't know. But I am going to find out. The lattice-work of intertwined branches and whole trees can be revealed in all its beauty come winter. A specialised job creating hedges for the Old English. So you find plenty of fellows named "Hedges".

Hedges can grow in parts as high as their constituent trees. Like the Normandy bocage, which was such a nightmare for our Fathers, a real nightmare for British and American troops to attack in. I believe that large fields are only the norm in places like Lincolnshire and other places where land has been "recently" reclaimed from the sea. The Fens, to be precise. I truly wish that you were here. We could just walk along the many public fields to look out at the view. Oh, we share so much. And, Sue, as you know, it's not only history in the hedgerows and the ancient trees in the woods, but the history you can feel beneath every mound, every ridge in the fields. We are right for each other. I cannot write. I long to sit with you and talk..."

He could have said so much more about those hedgerows. Poor Sue. He had already said quite enough! They were a patchwork, of fascinating historical time periods, divided by beautiful flora and lively fauna. He heard from the landlady that Hunts meet regularly. He never saw any though. That would have been a sight from Olde England. He looked out from the bedroom window of his bed and breakfast and merely saw the tall Stuart chimney stacks of their neighbour Grange Farm. These tall and thick hedgerows cut out virtually all traffic noise from the unseen roads as well. The rows divide and isolate, create a verdant screen behind which these farmers live.

He realised too how the seasons must have governed people's lives. Everything changed. For him the change was so quick, especially with confusing clock-changing 'twixt winter and summer. That was weird, man. It seemed like the days were longer by an hour each month. The seasons brought so many changes. Then the night-sky itself made him feel strange.

Norfolk was beautiful. He hired a motor dinghy for a couple of days and cruised the rivers and Broads. How he wished that he had a knowledgeable companion to identify the flora and fauna that dazzled him in it's diversity. Camping secretly on a marshy island he thought of that long ago day with Gideon on that huge African lake. There the talk had been of human rights, and struggles that might be. Here he was alone with his dreams of things that had been, of principles long ago established, and futures formed. He was more at peace now. He was a child of what had been. He could soak up the being of what it was that had formed those people of long ago.

To gaze at a ditched mound on a green heath, and imagine. Causeways over the ditch, barbaric splendor flaring as a cloak flames to reveal a garish tunic. Torchlight down a rutted lane, huts , family groupings immersed in the firelight tasks, of make and mend, of storytelling from afar... And then one blinks. And there is the mound, just a mound, in the midst of a ploughed field. Yes, Stephan. Only that sort of imagination makes my life worth living...

He began visiting the Cathedral cities and little market towns. Norwich with it's pebbled market place and stalls set out under the castle walls. An almost mediaeval experience of hucksters and pilgrims winding their way up through the lanes to the Cathedral cloisters. He checked. Not pilgrims. Camera festooned tourists.

From Norfolk he skirted The Wash, redolent of dreams and fortunes lost, and gazed across to the soft tranquil beauty of Lincolnshire, its own low green wooded Wolds.The Cathedral high on it's ridge, visible over many miles of lowlands. Staring up at the towering architecture he believed that he felt something of the faith those architects, stone-masons, and, yes, even labourers, had felt as they laboured on a project dedicated to God's glory, but the completion of which neither they, nor their sons, would ever see.

He would never tire of all the varied villages he passed through and sometimes stopped in. They were different in each Shire. The layout could be around a Saxon Green with perhaps a pond, or else strung out along a high street by the Danes. The buildings too were all different, both in style and in the local materials they were built of. The names that told of the first settlers, and even their race. He took detours off the main roads wherever he could, loving the detailed signposts at every turning or crossroads. He had long had a pretty detailed map of England in his head, and as a bushman he always knew which direction he was pointed in.

He crossed the Humber and followed the road north, crossing the high moors of Yorkshire, and into the Dales. Here perhaps he felt most at home. The softer hedgerows gave way to drystone walling. The expanse of moor was broken by smooth eroded rock. A rougher harder Cornwall. He revelled in the freedom and emptiness of it all. He visited the castles, the ruined abbeys. But they did not sing to his soul in the way that the wastes and moors ever could or even the old village houses had.

Buildings only began again to appeal to him when he reached the Northumbrian/Scots Borders. The peel towers set on the inaccessible crags, the fortified bastle houses of the middling folk; the village houses which surrounded a green onto which all the stock could be driven in times of danger. The houses set close together so that hurdles could be dropped between them, creating a fortified mass of houses. Strong bastles were at intervals, perhaps a peel tower at one end, below the earthworks of a Norman mote and bailey castle. So much like the wooden laagers of wagons he knew so much of. But this was set in stone, permanent, a record of the way his forefathers had lived. In the middle of the green the little village church. A dull grey stone, as all English churches had been left since Henry VIII and Cromwell's minions had passed by, relieved only by it's aspiring architecture and those glorious stained glass windows. And within the plaque, in so many such churches, to The Honoured Dead. Men and women bearing his name on all of them. Then he prayed. He felt that he had come home. To a windswept, eroded, rough land. A naked land, unprotected. A land that bred the men he believed in.

He knew that he was descended from a Border clan. A surname. He knew the old tales of rough men and equally tough women.

Folk living on the edge. Their wealth precarious, their pride their all. As with their surname. As with modern Mafia gangsters; allow that to be tarnished and you were lost. Never suffer a blow without returning it two-fold.

Stand up for your kin. All for one. One for all. But no romance. Just a hard, backbreaking, struggle to survive both the country and those who lived in it. Not only the Scots. Their own kind as well. Moments of glory. Solway Moss. Flodden Field. The Hanging Stone. He searched them all out. Looked. Imagined. Walked the Wall. The moors. Felt himself seeing the high unbroken formidable line not from the top as a Roman legionnaire, but from the bottom, looking on. The best light horsemen in the world. From Brigantii in their chariots, to horsed Reivers. From their cruel way of life came so many words in English such as blackmail, or phrases like hot trod – not romantic words as he saw now, looking at the drab ruins of their dwellings. Simply words reflecting their lives on the Border. He had tried to imagine what had made them what they were. Now he had an inkling.

Once, he told himself, this had been true of much of his native land; from the wild untamed weald in the south to here in the north. A land for real men and woman who, like his Father, worked the unreliable soil and defended his own. But still created their own world of dreams and myth which enthralled them at night with tales around the campfire. A green beautiful world, the greenness a result of continuous rain which caused disease, landslides, and crop-failure. A deadly beauty indeed.

He could picture those men and women who had lived in and worked this land. The landscape told their story for them. The names of lost Kingdoms flickered through his mind. He knew the constantly shifting borders of each. Of The Black Douglas. The Moray Forth dividing the southern and Northern Picts. Edinburgh and Arthur's Seat. Of Strathclyde, Rheged, Bernicia and Deira; the twin Kingdoms which united in Northumbria, stretched to Edinburgh. Of Rheged which had almost but not

113

quite pushed the invading English into the sea at Bamburgh. He heard the haunting words of The Goddodin, that vain expedition by the glorious 300 which had set out from Edin's Rock to perish at Catterick. Soon thereafter the Rock At Dun Edin was a Northumbrian English fastness.

He saw the ordinary people in his mind's eye. The priest hard at work in his scriptorium, the farmer in his fields. Not only the weather to watch for but always the raiding war-band. The people who had soon become so intertwined through marriage, alliances, and of course rape, that after a few centuries they were of one blood; only the histories and languages of their rulers defining them as Angle or Briton, even Scot or Pict. Romans and their Frankish auxiliaries had settled this land. Scots and Picts had come as raiders or prisoners-of-war, as foederati to both Roman and Briton.

Then had arrived the Norse Vikings, with their Danish kinsmen to the south. British Strathclyde had survived through both its military prowess and diplomatic skills until the eleventh century, and English Bernicia too had fought off the Danes.

When Scot and English finally divided Strathclyde the modern borders of the two realms that were to dominate Britain emerged. The rulers might have called themselves by different national names, but the people of the Border lands were of much the same stock, and when Edward I unleashed his wars of conquest any hope of their lives becoming being even comprehensible to our own were swept away.

These were the lawless centuries, with all the bloodshed, hardship, and personal grief that entails.

The Wall. Hadrian's Wall. Stark on the moors. He walked most of its length, his mind a camera.

He turned his back on the stark bastles and lonely Peel Towers, and made his way south through the beautiful loveliness of the

Lake District. Here he found peace. He rambled, climbed the fells, found beauty in the landscape and in the bosom of the lakes themselves. The green beauty that comes with frequent soft rain, contrasting with the harsh windswept beauty of the stony moors. He rambled the spine of England, down the Pennines. He regretted he had not the time or money to explore either Scotland or Wales. He crossed the Derbyshire Peak district. Again the high moors drew him, called to him. He gazed up at the castles high on their rock-girt summits, wondered at standing stones and circles. Tried to understand the societies that had erected them.

To Shropshire. The great barrier of Offa's Dyke. The gentleness of the Stipple Stones and the Welsh Border country after the harsh north. But he knew that it was not so. He knew of the brutal wars that had led to that dyke, and which had not ceased because of it. Here he felt those long-ago myths of Arthurian legend and believed them, even more so than he had in the west Country. Not the high romance of a Chrétien de Troy, but of a deserted soldier fighting for an idea. A figure perhaps more true to the brutality of the Welsh Saints' lives than to a hero of high chivalry.

He returned to London, lost in dreams. To sell his car, say goodbye to no-one except a phone-call to a surprised uncle. An aeroplane, a love reborn. A chance to talk with Pa. He would understand. He had felt those ideas in a desert hell, and on Italy's hostile shores. For the Youth England was again an idea, a green beauty to remember and visualise in places far away. He thought of Tolkien's Shire. A land to be believed in, to be fought for, a hope and a light in the darkness of his world. Home is NOT where the heart is...

He thought of Sue as the plane took off. She would be back by now. Would she, during her long tour of Europe, have felt as he did? Would she understand?

Chapter Nine

The Student

Sue was there, waiting for him. She understood.

She had felt the two-way pull as he had done. They were drawn closer. He was off to 'varsity down south soon. She spent a lot of time at the house on the hill. The three of them, the defiantly young Judy, Sue, and he, spent a lot of time in the Bush. Just rambling. Loosely. His rifle slung over his shoulder. He took her to all his favourite places. And the brief restraint that had grown up between them faded. They marveled anew at the flora and fauna. He showed her the watering hole where he and Gideon had spent so many hours in the early dawn light observing the wild creatures of the Bush. It was there, on a soft bank of grass shaded by an acacia tree, that they first loved each other. They were children of the Bush. This was their home. Yes, he would go away for a while. But he was committed now. Neither questioned that.

Sue and Judy got on like a house on fire. The little bitch, defying her years, scrambled all over her, smothering her with kisses. The "one-man-dog" had found another soul-mate. He loved watching them play. At times Sue asked about Gideon. He found himself talking in the past tense. Oh, they wrote. But more gossip now than about ideas he realised for the first time. They visited the village and Gideon's parents together. The Old Man seemed slightly more reserved than before. He put it down to his absence, his growing older, to Gideon not being there.

But Sue was more thoughtful as they left. She even seemed more protective. She was not to mention Gideon again. He was to remember that later.

It was now late summer. He had left England in autumn and returned to an African spring in all it's verdant beauty. Soon it would be Christmas and then 'varsity.

It was a quiet Christmas. Sue went back home to spend it with her family. He wandered alone. No Gideon. No Sue. He looked afresh at his home. He knew that he loved this place, these views. Here he knew the name of all the plants and grasses and trees that grew, of everything that crawled, wriggled, walked. Of course, not all of them in English.

The time for his departure for 'varsity grew closer. He had chosen a middle way. Had his draft deferred. Neither taken the gap and left the country permanently nor got his military service over with. It hung over him, his personal sword of Damocles. He had made his choice however. He was coming home. Sue would be there. She was going to do a nursing course at the local teaching hospital, but he would visit her.

The years that followed were to stay in his mind in flashes, still images. His heart was to be far away, but never was his mind to be so stimulated, nor, truth to be told, was his body. The years passed like a dream, not touching the reality back home. He was completely alone again. As at school, living in his mind.

The drive was the first thing. Thousands of miles in the little yellow Anglia. A time of solitude, transition. Not the experience of later years in which a group of drunken but happy students he was to meet would pile in and dare each other to drive the whole way without stopping, spelling each other at the wheel. No, this was his thing. When he drove quietly through the ever-changing landscapes of Africa; from grassland over wide rivers into hill-country with hidden ravines, through one-horse towns with their broad avenues lined by a few houses and shops, a church, all baking in the sun. Then after wide plateaux he climbed high mountains, skirted semi-deserts and saw little hamlets off the road set in scrub and dried brown grass. Over twisting mountain passes and swooping down again into endless plains. He slept under the stars, in lay-by's and under canvass. He gloried in sunrise and sunset, the wild flowers of the little Karroo and Kalahari in the lushness of the great plains. He slowed as groups of springbok crossed the road, glimpsed klipspringer and baboons on rocky outcrops, and listened to the sounds of the night and the high-pitched hyena. It was a special time. His time as he prepared himself for the urban jungle that lay ahead. The ideas that he would encounter, accept, argue, and reject or accept.

He had been here before. But then apartheid had never really touched him. He had been a bystander. Now he would really begin to contrast the life he enjoyed with those of an artificially excluded people.

The final part of his journey was on an eight lane highway, piercing directly through the suburban sprawl. Only at the last did he begin the climb the slopes of the great mountain rising up directly from the sea, towards his student res. He curved in through the gates, parked, and walked to admin. A hale and hearty bloke greeted him and introduced himself in an exaggerated local accent. "Hoosit, ou maat," he called out. "Another blerry colonial." He looked askance at the new student's number plates. "Leave yer things in that old heap and come along to the admin. block." There he was quickly sorted out, and given the keys to one of the little rooms in a block like all the others. Built for returning soldiers at the end of World War Two, and as permanent now as they had been temporary then, the res. The res. consisted of a dozen such blocks, each containing up to a dozen rooms opening out onto a wide verandah, with ablution blocks set at either end. His new acquaintance, Rob, showed him along to his home for the next few years, and helped him bring over his things from the car.

"Hey, right now you are lucky, Jong. You got space to park. But you are going to have to work your times out later." He remembered the terraced housing in London with their eagerly sought-after on-street parking. He was fortunate. His window opened onto the mountain slopes. A little off to his left, beyond a freeway, he could spy the main campus. The furniture in the room was sparse, and unlike more local youths he had little of his own to add, excepting a picture or two. There was a bed, "Don't worry so," said his new-found friend. "Big enough for two when your back gets the hang of it!" A cupboard, bedside table, chair, and desk.

Hey, this was great. His own space. Rob left him with a cheery invite to the pub later that evening "after his first dose of mass poisoning" in the dining-room. He began unpacking, giving that room a personal touch within minutes. Still not tired, despite the long day's drive and all he had experienced since arriving in the streets of the big City, he smoked a quick fag and then looked at his watch. Time for the dining-room, according to the pamphlet given him and all the other new residents.

He walked in to be met by a loud greeting from Rob, who introduced him to his mates at the long mess-tables. "Come over here – I'll introduce you to the Maitre de Hotel." This was a portly black African gentleman with an air of obvious authority. "Make sure that you never fall out with this chap," whispered Rob.

"He runs the whole show and keeps the res. drinks and food bills whenever you want anything extra or hope to invite a friend. He can make or break a relationship!" The old codger grinned and took the hand the new student thrust out.

"Hey, no need to upstage the rest of yer mates!" cried Rob. Still, the new student was left with a good feeling by the grin and hearty pump the man in authority gave him.

There was rather a plethora of foodstuffs. Comestibles as his school chums would have called it when in a Billy Bunter mood.

The main courses were good, but his hand was rather lightly tapped by one of the coloured women behind the counter when he did an Oliver Twist. "Hmm, got to work on that one," he thought to himself.

Then down the pub with his new crowd. The place was exactly like the pubs he had known in England. And there were more like this he was assured. But the beer was all African Lager. Strong pints of draught lager that went down quickly in the heat. The newcomer was decidedly light-headed by the time he was helped, laughing, to a car. His schoolday experiences were going to get him through here alright.

He was tall, broad-shouldered, handsome, with a strong square jaw and long sideburns offsetting his shoulder length hair. It was rich and fell in waves. His face – where not covered in hair - was tanned a deep Colonial mahogany, in which his green eyes glinted merrily.

He had a couple of days. Days spent in registering for this, that and the other, for individual courses and clubs. He soon fell in with other faces grown familiar from queue after queue. His social life was centring. He began to fall in with his drinking and socializing friends of the years to come.

They were different though. These students lived in an affluent, another alien world of innocent inquiry and unknowing brutality, of pretensions and intolerance... They were not African. They would have been as much at home in London as the great city in which they lived.

He found himself becoming two people and living two completely separate lives. He found fun with the hale and hearty thoughtless rugger types who lived in res. and who took courses like Engineering, who rarely had a thought in their heads, unless it was objectionable, racist, and rude. With them he played, enjoyed camping out in the tame Bush on the City margins. He met girls in their set, drank cheap red wine, and gallons of strong beer in the summer heat. The City's pubs and bars were his haunts of an evening. And often still in the morning.

He experimented with marijuana and reverted to booze. He would arrive late and disheveled in his lecture halls and eat his breakfast in the back row. He found that he was not exceptionally clever, and had to go into hiding from his friends when the time came to write essays, sit tests, or write exams.

He still sought out fellows to talk things through with. This was his second persona. It was at such times he grew closer to a chap his own age called Chris. A local chap, he was tall and slim, well-built and good-looking. A great one for the girls, he played guitar and sang like a pro at gigs and in bars for a few bucks most nights after the short 'varsity days. He was the man without politics, only aversions, who lived his life and said fuck the rules of his Anglo Saxon society. Most of his girls were Mediterranean types, and his short romances wafted him off on fantasies and imaginings that would dominate his life. He was fun to be with, but perhaps he and his circle were a bit too intellectually demanding. The Student found himself acting out a role with them that was not easy. He enjoyed the talk of philosophy, it was after all one of his minors. But their artificial constructs and superficial discussions always made him more seemingly aware of the real questions in the society he had found himself.

Soon he found himself enjoying the times when he could get Chris on his own. Without his pretentious friends. Oh, he knew that he would never be in Chris's inner circle, but after a while he found himself in a separate one. The two young men found that they had a lot in common, despite so much that they could never interest the other in. For the northerner all this talk of ideas, of customs, cultures, mores, philosophies, and ideas generally, led directly to the world he was in. Chris simply did not connect. He was interested in the world as an individual, saw no place for himself getting involved with the wider picture. Just as the Student saw everything in terms of it being somewhere along a historical continuum, time-line, call it what you will, Chris saw it in isolation. Practical, there, and real.

He was almost totally apolitical. He had grown up in a very English suburb of the City, and it was that constricting life style that he was trying to escape. He rejected practically every aspect of Anglo Saxon culture, without fully realizing that it itself had created him and it was through that prism that he saw his world.

Foreign foods, foreign music, foreign girls. Oh yes, foreign exotic girls. Chris's natural gift for languages allowed him any number of times to butt in successfully to girls' conversations. The whiff of a Mediterranean accent set him off like a beagle. He was utterly incorrigible. Life with him as a friend was to be often left as a lonely wall fly. No hassle. It was just one of those hopelessly ill-fitting relationships which the Student was always getting into. Their coming-together always meant that each held back. In a way the Student felt in awe of Chris and his sophisticated easy ways. Yet in his turn Chris seemed to admire his friend's book-learning and general knowledge. Their discussions never went off at a tangent.

True, Chris had grown up with his world. He could accept much of what he saw, and still reach out. For the Student it was not that easy. He had been there before, true. But not lived the life. Not woken up to headlines which assumed the reader knew about pass-laws and segregation, about which areas of the City were for whites, coloureds, or blacks. Little everyday things which were taken for granted in this society constantly took him aback. It was a second culture-shock.

Again, choices. He had, ironically, decided on a Liberal Arts degree, majoring in History and Philosophy, with English and Archaeology as minors. There he could not divorce theory from reality. His lecturers and professors were predominantly liberals themselves. The students included many committed to the struggle. And the campus was not all white either. People of all religions and hues thronged the Students' Union. Here he did not find people of Gideon's stamp. These he met on his own level. He was never to become true friends with any black, coloured, or Asian students. He frequently wondered why, but managed to quiet the question with the thought that to befriend a man simply because of his race was itself racist. But he knew himself too well for that. He knew the truth. And it disquieted him.

Still, the thoughts, the philosophy, the exposure to daily life in such an unreal society, would lead him to becoming an active protestor. Deep down this was not a result of classroom theorising, but of his boyhood upbringing. He had to take a stand. He began to think it through... And made his choices.

Hey, man, This is not cricket. I'm English. So fight the good fight, for the right, there are absolutes, and individual rights are among them. Fuck the State. All good liberals are rebels anyway. Believe in God, love your fellow man, and go, man, GO! The church is behind us, and The Man is still there behind me all the way. Fuck THEM. The beat is cool. The lager is cool, the cars are souped-up, and the birds hang out.

And hell, man, the Surf Is Up!

For Real, man! The beaches were great. And at res. his friends introduced him to places neither his parents nor their friends would ever have known of. They included a couple of nudist beaches a little way off the beaten track but quite accessible to athletic students. Take a friend, preferably female, park your buggy, slip and slide hand over hand down the rocks, and slide down the scree to a sandy white cove. On a good day, watch the naked youngsters cavorting on the beach, join in, let nature guide the two of you to a sheltered spot. But watch out for the pearly white arse of a burly policeman – not exactly in plain clothes, but certainly standing out from the crowd.

O.K. That was the good side that came later. The horrible truth of the first time he followed his mates down to the beach was somewhat different. Too shy to join in the ball-play on the sand, he found himself lying for hours on his stomach in the blazing summer sun, apart from a quick cooling dip in the sea. For the rest he lay and watched, quietly digging his own little hole in the sand. After a few hours his back felt raw. But only when he had dressed furtively and made his way back up to where he had left his car did the true consequences reveal themselves. He was barely able to put his raw and tender backside on the hot plastic of the driving seat. Driving home was itself agony, but was only to grow worse over the next few days. As for getting up to lectures and sitting on a hard seat, that was out of the question for a long while. Oh hell. And did he get sympathy from his mates? Did he hell! It was all he could do to live it down without garnering an indecent nickname!

Then his first real girl experience at 'varsity, the time a rich socialite type he had long been casual friends with, asked him around to her place. Her boyfriend was a medical student who worked longer hours than most of their set. Often he found himself alone with her in the pub. On one hot sultry summer's afternoon following a few drinks she had asked him. She had a pool.

She led his Anglia in her black BMW. They drove along a winding mountain road to one of the most exclusive suburbs. The gates were electronic. The house was built in the style of a mock eighteenth century Dutch colonial mansion, set in beautifully landscaped gardens.

This was plain intimidating. He parked behind her car on the gravel drive. She swung out of her car, her long hair swinging, and said "Right, the pool is in back over here".

There was, naturally, a poolside bar. She fixed him a drink and whilst he stood there bemused she said she would "Pop off for a moment".

He stood there, glass in hand, facing a spectacular view of the mountain range behind, the slopes covered in pine forest. Behind him this glorious mansion. Above him a deep blue sky. He wanted out. Now.

But then she re-appeared, wrapped in a towel.

"Nobody home, she said. It's the servant's day off. I did tell the house-keeper I was taking a swim with a friend, and I don't think she'll disturb us. So what do you say, shall we simply enjoy our swim in full freedom?"

With that she dropped the towel, pirouetted, and dived into the water.

She was completely naked. She was beautiful. Perfectly tanned, long legs, flat stomach, perfect little breasts. Hell, he looked long and hard in those few seconds. Then he was tearing off his clothes and diving in after her. He finally caught up with her at the shallow end. She turned and came to him. Her nipples stood proudly. He had stopped thinking for once in his life. Now he simply took what was on offer. He cupped her tight little bottom in his hands and raised her to him. She had shaven all her body-hair. He had never really seen a girl's fanny before. She was lovely. So round, so smooth. He had an open canvass on which he began to practice all those arts learnt long ago from those little black girls back on the farm.

She shuddered, again and again. "Come," she said. "Quickly."

She enveloped him with her legs, locking him to her, half-floating in the blue water, locking him to her as she guided him inside of her. He had never "gone all the way" before. Now it simply happened. Naturally. Beautifully.

They spent the next hour swimming, sunbathing, fondling each other. Then he had to leave. Her folks would be back home soon.

They saw each other after that. They talked. Yet never again was he invited back to her place. That afternoon had been it. A memory. Che sera sera. It was a fantasy drive back to res.

Life in res. was fun. And there it was that he worked and met friends. Most of the chaps were brash and often brilliant. They introduced him to a lifestyle he had never known before. A lifestyle that rarely appeared in his regular letters to Sue. Not that he kept any secrets from her. Rather, he simply left things out. Such as the impromptu parties, the uncomfortable sex in a narrow bunk-bed when he had managed to smuggle a girlfriend in. Life was easy, man. There was never any commitment. No guilt. He played hard, he worked hard.

As never before. Never had he been so stretched. And it still all seemed so unreal. Starting with the very air he breathed. The cool Mediterranean climate compared to the harsh extremes of Home, the mild winters and cool summers so lovely on the beach. The evenings talking late with a lager in hand. The barbecues in the mountainside forests complete with a crate of cheap wines. Life was good. Life was cool. But hell, life was also weird.

Because those long evening chats led to a deeper political commitment than he had ever known before. He found himself throwing in his lot with the struggle. He became an active protester, something his rather aloof friend Chris denigrated but rarely felt committed enough to try to talk him out of. He skipped going home one year – too far, too expensive – and spent his holidays earning money through odd retail jobs (he made himself very popular once by working in a Kentucky Fried Chicken joint, making sure that he fried up an extra batch on 11.45 sharp just before closing. The rule was that all the previous day's food should be chucked out. It was. Into his car boot. His room became rather a popular number in the res. that vac. with the other exiles. So the world he was in became his world to a far greater degree than he had expected. Mostly though he went home. Either drove or flew.

The years had their own time-table. The seasons coincided with starting courses, enjoying the excitement of discovery and research, then the pain and, for him, relentless pain, of writing out the research, studying for the examinations. Then he went out of circulation. He had to study hard to pass. He knew that. His education had cost his folk's a lot. He knew that. Just as he knew that without working as hard as he could he might fail.

When he did go home he had little time to relax and join in daily life. He spent his time mainly with his folks, and with Sue. He met Stephan more whilst at home than he did at 'varsity. The medical students lived almost a different life, more attached to the Teaching Hospital. But they stayed close friends. He and Sue got on very well, as always.

Whilst at 'varsity he and Sue had exchanged letters so very frequently. Sometimes she had written daily. The letters would sometimes arrive together and he would have to endure a lot of "chaffing" from his mates as he carried the bundle back to his room. They wrote about everything. Whenever they had something to say, whenever they did something, achieved something, failed at something, felt in need of reassurance, or whenever they missed each other. They began to know each other through their letters in a way few other couples ever could. Oh, their correspondence was punctuated by phone-calls, and weeks at a time when he was home. Often though his leave never exactly coincided with hers, especially when she began work as a probationer. But when they did meet there was never any real adjustment to be made.

That first holiday, however, he drove north, right up to her place. The drive was as varied as ever. But it took so long and he wanted to spend every moment he had with his loved ones, in his place. In fact, he convinced Mother it was cheaper to fly than to drive the car, if wear-and-tear, petrol, and hotels were all added up.

Her folks were polite but not effusive. They seemed to accept what the two youngsters had going and respected it. Whilst there he took her to their first Drive-In cinema together.

The screen was a huge erection on a slight rise, surrounded by many acres of enclose fenced-in land. Within that enclosure there were rows of rounded humps with a road between each. There were posts with speakers on delineating each parking space. Towards the centre of the complex was a sort of mini-market, selling all sorts of confectionary and other goodies.

You drove in, and if you had arrived early enough, chose your hump with what you considered the best view of the screen, wound down the driver's window, and hooked the speaker up to the car. Then you hoped that the weather was kind.

Of course, many of the younger clients had no interest in either hearing or seeing the film. There they were, in a confined but very private car, parked as far away from the old fogeys as possible. Perfect. Theirs were the cars with the windows very fogged up.

Sue's father, on hearing of their outing, looked very approvingly at his little car, with it's narrow back seat. No room for much hanky-panky there, he thought.

Well, he had underestimated a true bushman.

They drove up to the little kiosk, paid for their tickets. When he drove past the screen, heading for the outer perimeter, Sue made no comment. He parked halfway up the little hump and, before attaching the speaker, asked her if there was anything she wanted from the shop.

"No," she said. "I think I have what I want just here."

He looked at her. Reached over. This was a dream come true. She kissed him. He slid his hand up her rumpled skirt.

She said, "Wait a moment," and raised her bottom, sliding her panties down and undoing her top, loosened her bra. He began to fondle her using all those old tricks. She thrust her pelvis against his hand. These were no longer tricks. This was not a game. This was his girl. He loved her. He would do anything he knew to make her happy. Keep her and hold her. For ever. She had never experienced anything like this before. She shuddered at last, fell back against the cheap plastic seat.

"Darling, can I...?"

"Yes," he said, showing her how. Her lips were soft, her tongue that of a little witch.

They never did remember the name of that movie. They remembered that Drive-In cinema for the rest of their lives.

He loved that car.

Later on they travelled down to his home together, stopping overnight with an elderly aunt of hers. Her father had tried to think of everything. His parents gave them both a lot more latitude.

At home he took her to all his boyhood haunts. She shared his cave. There they made love, and in the Bush by firelight, under the stars of the cloudless African sky. He told her of how he had felt when first he saw her tumbled back at school, her dress up around her waist, her long brown legs reaching right up to her panties. Short little pants, somewhat awry, with little fronds peeking out. Oh, he had long had wet dreams about them. His first girl. She really had him going sexually from the word go. And now those legs, all of her, were his. As he was hers. They delighted in exploring each other's bodies, tried any new trick they could think of. The Bush gave them a lot of scope as well as having its obvious limitations though. That was where another of Gideon's sisters came in. The people understood these things. They were shown a hut discretely set aside from the village. They were shown the sign that the hut would be available. Their love-life, in all it's manifestations, blossomed.

Later, when he flew back, car-less, he and Sue rarely left his home unless Pa or a friend drove them someplace. They spent a lot of time in the Bush with Judy, talking about the future, their future. Somehow they spent less and less time at her place. With the distances involved it was certainly easier to base themselves at one of the two farm-houses. Sue also knew that her bloke and her parents were never going to be close. They tolerated each other, even respected each other, but they were too different. In politics, in philosophy, in every conceivable way. They thought the youngster a tearaway, without respect or common-sense. There was always the possibility of a quarrel. Something Sue did her best to avoid. So it was not her private childhood world they explored, but his. And they made it theirs. She brought her imagination and her love of life to everything on the farm, especially to the cave. There they sat, close, sharing the view, each other's company and each other's thoughts.

The political scene was worsening, but somehow seemed so different from the situation he felt himself involved in down south. There seemed such a real chance of a settlement that would appeal to everyone. Both of them still saw their future in Africa, their Africa. When he was alone, however, he saw things differently. He could not entirely divorce the paternalistic self-interest of the colonials from the evils he saw and read about every day at 'varsity. Neither could Pa.

The old liberal was constantly asking his son to consider the alternatives. That had been his real motive, thought his boy, in sending him to England when he could not really afford to. Pa even raised it with Sue. Sue was rather hard-headed about it. No ways. This was her home, and this was where she wanted to live her life. England was all very well for a holiday, but theirs was not a life-style she wanted. Crabby little terraced houses, parking in the street, the claustrophobic cloudy skies. No way.

One year, a real madcap adventure developed when a bunch of colonial mates at res. got together to pool their resources to drive up north together. They talked about it for days. There was to be no stopping for sleep, just swapping drivers and leaving a trail of beer-cans in their wake. Oh, they got back alright, but for most it left them just as without transport as before, and for the unlucky driver it entailed three minor collisions with passing flora, one with mountain rocks, and two rather expensive tows. The unfortunate, with whom the Student identified closely, was disbarred from ever trying it again by his Pa...

Back at 'varsity the Student found himself responding to both his conscience and to peer pressure and joining in the student protests against apartheid. He started off not being quite serious. The system was absurd. Had to collapse soon. He could do bugger all anyway.

He would long remember his first demo on campus. They started off quite happily enough on the steps of the Uni., chanting slogans and waving happily at the reporters from the liberal press. What happened next was a shock.

Police cars and black Maria's came hurtling onto campus, their sirens giving off a banshee wail. People's mouths dropped open, The vans suddenly disgorged scores of policemen and what seemed like dozens of dogs. A few of the fainthearted stole away as best they could but the majority of students simply grew angrier. What the hell, this is MY place! Suddenly the sound of a megaphone cut through the loud impassioned talk. A policeman was reading the riot act. Disperse or else. The Student found anger welling up in his heart too. This was how they treated the blacks all the time. Well, not him.

"Not me," he whispered.

"Noways," said his chum from res. "I'll be behind you all the way." The joker. The apolitical who always saw humour in what was going on. The Student hardly heard him.

He clenched his fists and waited, counting out the seconds. The police charged. He fell to a swinging baton. Before he could fully understand what was happening to him he was lifted up by the armpits and flung in the back of a police van, into a tangle of youngsters, boys confused and the girls often crying. As soon as the van was full they were carted off to the station. There came the degrading business of identification, finger-printing, strip-searching, and finally his first few hours in a crowded prison cell.

That was his experience. And that of many others. His res. chum had opted for another route. Oh, he had kept his promise. He had promised to be behind the student all the way. He had stood behind his chum until the baton whistled down. Then he had crouched, seemingly oblivious to all the action around him, and whilst bent over began scanning the ground. The first line of officers passed him by. A follow-up constable asked the curious figure what it thought it was about, "Searching for my spectacles," came the answer "I dropped it in the maul."

Echoes from police college obviously still resonated in the constable's ears, because the next moment he joined in the search. All around was chaos but at it's center was a little circle of normalcy. When other officers asked, "What the bleery hell" their colleague was up to, and were told, they either laughed or joined in the futile search themselves. Finally, as the center of action moved further along the main avenue, the two youngsters, cop and student, straightened up, looked at each other, burst out laughing, and went their separate ways. It was a story to dine out on in years to come.

The Student's ordeal continued though. He was allowed one phone-call. He would always remember his Father's voice after he began the conversation by saying "I'm phoning from a police station". No questions. No "What did you do?" Merely a reassuring voice saying that he'd have a lawyer down there immediately. He did too. The lawyer soon had him out.

By this time the public outcry was too great for the authorities. These were white middle-class kids they had beaten up and arrested. The courts found that as the campus was private property onto which the police had not been invited. It was the police who were trespassing.

Huge damages were due. The students happily continued to line their verges adjoining the public roads; shouting slogans and waving their banners. In the end though that got a bit boring.

As for the young radical, he saw a local doctor and retired back to res. nursing a slightly cracked skull and an almighty headache. He also had a sense of real anti-climax. He was later to remember how he had felt as he grimly awaited that baton charge. Much as he would later, before going into action as a soldier.

From being rather a dilettante revolutionary he now threw himself whole-heartedly into the cause. What cause? Liberty and equality for all? No more indignity and oppression? We all suffer that. No. A free chance for all. He was no communist. He was a liberal, imbued with rose-tinted ideals, but he felt all the more for knowing it. It was his passion. He began taking around petitions and distributing leaflets in the suburbs. Often threatened, twice arrested, he learnt more about human nature than before. On one occasion, whilst out drinking one night with his mates he heard an uproar and turned around to see a black man cowering under a hail of baton blows from a policeman. He turned and despite the appeals of his chums "It's no use", "Let it go!", he ran to grab the policeman's arm.

"Come on," he said, "he is in no state to do anything. Please let him be."

"Fuck you," said the burly cop, "you fucking well get in too!"

In the van he checked the black man's wounds. No real damage as far as he could see (this was also a scene that he would remember). He asked his name and what had been the reason for the police attack.

"No reason, man," said the other. "I just didn't have the necessary permits to be there."

"Shite," thought the Boy. "What will happen now?"

"I'll get locked up for a few months, my family will get no money, and you will be out in an hour or two, whitey," said the other, purposefully misunderstanding him.

And that was how it was. This time he did not even have to telephone his long-suffering family long-distance. He was simply given a warning. He had yet again seen the brute force of the authorities. In the opinion of the sergeant he needed no further lesson.

But he did. Most of the students on campus simply heard the protests as background music, but the cause was beginning to be a part of the Student's life. Oh, he still loved his fun. His idea of a good time was as it had been during his first year at university. He had learnt those lessons well. Yet he remembered his Father saying something, once, during his last vac. about being glad that he was "doing the right thing". He would not let his Father, or their shared principles, down.

His beliefs, however, were still largely those derived from his youthful reading, from hearing the small black community on their farm struggling to do "justice", ideas shared with his Father. He had never made real friends among the radical students. In fact to a large extent he rejected their socialism. He believed firmly in empowering the individual. Never in terms of distinct groups or classes. His Mother had been an evangelical Christian, and had taken him to church. He had never really got into the "speaking tongues", "Hallelujah" type of worship he grew up with.

His Father spoke little of his religious beliefs, as opposed to his social and political views. That was one private corner in his Father. Perhaps it stemmed from an agreement with his Mother from way-back-when.

Mother's social life revolved around her church, so Father had simply escorted her there. He largely ignored the other worshippers, and even the Student could see that that was because he felt ill-at-ease in their company, and he knew that Father would never want to be impolite or rude to Mother's friends. That was just "not on". But once he had caught Father alone in the car-park outside the church building. Father was having a smoke. By this time they were already on first name terms.

"What is up?" he asked his Father, who seemed to be quietly having a fit. "Son," said his Father, if you ever find yourself taking characters like that too seriously, simply read the gospels. Find out for yourself how they manage to get it so wrong. They never remember that the New Testament was just that."

But the Student had never bothered to spend much time reading the gospels or any other part of the New Testament. He had other things in his life. He found himself rejecting his Mother's church, and drifted into a state which was not even definite enough to be called "Agnostic". God and religion was something he knew was there, but he rarely even thought about it.

There was a strong fundamentalist Christian tradition in his new city though. He had wandered into their churches from time to time in the first few years of his stay in res. He found that they harbored the most despicable racists in their midst. Far more than even back home. The grim Old Testament, God of the chosen few was rammed home. The white man was His. The sons of Cain were the blacks. Prayers were offered for those brave boys of theirs who were upholding civilization and God's cause on the Borders. Terrorists equalled blacks equalled communists equalled the destruction of civilization as we knew it. Everything he despised was thrown at him from one pulpit after another.

"Fucking hypocrites." He had experienced "white civilisation" first hand. "I know," he said to himself.

Then came the appeal to join in a demo down the main street of the City. Posters were stuck up on the Students' Union walls, people discussed it in the Union, pubs, and homes. For once even the engineers and sportsmen felt strongly. They knew that the authorities were going to take this seriously, and that any attempt to march on the heart of the City was going to meet trouble. This was not the campus, where the students had a measure of invulnerability.

There was an air of unease as they gathered. A lot of people laughed too loudly at nothing. They looked for their friends. It was an atmosphere he was to learn to know too well. They set off. Stragglers fell by the wayside, but others joined. They were to meet up with trades-union leaders and a worker's march in the main street of the City. The press were everywhere on their flanks. Most motorists hooted in support as they marched along the wide pavements. A few shouted curses and imprecations. The jostling crowd began to loosely form formations, banners waving high in front. Their spirits lifted. They began to sing freedom hymns. "We shall overcome, SOMEDAY..." They sang. The mood changed again as they left the freeway and descended down through the meaner suburban streets, a part of Town where few of the middle-class students had ever actually walked through before. They moved closer together, their songs and chants becoming more defiant.

Then, as the street became wider and they began to approach the junction with main street, just beyond the Anglican Cathedral, they saw them.

A tight disciplined phalanx of policemen, with helmets and full riot gear, but now far more terrifying were the armed men on the flanks, ready to open fire. Many of the protestors had themselves been conscripts in the army or in the police. These young men understood all too clearly what stood between them and their hoped for peaceful march through the City centre. The girls among them understood too.

The leaders hesitated. The banners drooped, then swung up. The demonstration looked for all the world like a march once more.

Then the loudspeakers. The riot act being read. And suddenly the marchers disintegrated. Men and women, the supposed leaders, fell in agony under a hail of plastic bullets, and their comrades were quickly overwhelmed by clouds of tear gas, through which charged the baton and whip-wielding police. No quarter this time. No time for cameos and momentary interludes. Those shot or gassed were being efficiently dispatched to waiting police vans. Those scattering in terror were not simply being arrested but were being quite deliberately beaten first.

The Student had been near the front. He could have sworn he heard the order given to fire. He saw the gas coming toward him like a cloud and heard the crack of batons, the shrieks of the victims. He turned and ran to escape that billowing cloud. Anywhere. Just to get away. He saw a large building, it's doors open. He saw others running towards it. He ran as hard as he could. He heard students shout "Sanctuary!" and more and more followed. After awhile the noise outside began to abate and he saw men in long gowns rushing to close the double doors through which he had entered.

Silence fell. A weird silence. He looked around. He was in the echoing, aching, quiet of what he now recognized as the Cathedral. The Anglican Cathedral which he had so often passed but had only been inside once, as a curious sightseer. The men who had closed the doors were priests. Priests dressed in cassocks. He giggled. This was living history!

Gathering his wits he looked around him. There must have been a hundred or more students, both men and women, boys and girls, in that place. He could not understand why the police had not followed them in. They were later to hear that although the old law of Sanctuary had never been repealed, that had not of course stopped the police. No. It was for a far more pragmatic, if not as romantic, a reason. After their experience on campus the police were loath to enter where the authorities clearly refused them entry. And this the Bishop had loudly done, using a voice trained to public speaking which rivaled any loudspeaker.

"These children have claimed sanctuary in God's house," he proclaimed. "I will not allow one of them to be taken out against their own free will."

And the police listened.

And so began the siege.

At first there was chaos. Not of biblical proportions. Everybody was confused, asking. Because of the place most were whispering however. Uncertainty was everywhere. Until the Bishop and his canons returned from standing guard outside. They began organizing refugees, talking to people. Spontaneously they all began to pray. The Student huddled in the corner, listening, willing himself to join in. Somehow his sense of individuality held him back from the pack. But he listened, he watched. Said little.

Soon the logistics were sketched out. Toilets and basic hygiene sorted. Food was smuggled in quite openly, although students trying to leave were rapidly picked up by the police cordon.

With organisation people began to feel free to express themselves. Each one had their own little space. A sort of society in miniature developed. Entertainments began to be organised. Of course nobody knew how long they would remain in their predicament. But the power lines remained uncut, and soon the telephone lines to friends and family were humming. Lawyers began marshalling.

And all the while the Cathedral tried to continue with its own separate life. The Student heard and saw the hauntingly beautiful hymns and ancient liturgies being sung. He experienced a way of worship so different from that of his youth. Nobody preached at him. No-one forced their views on him. He was free in there, free in a way he had rarely been.

Oh, he knew that if it had not been due to weird circumstances he would not be there. He was a prisoner, he knew that. But the sedate worship, the tradition, the beauty, all called out to him. This was an integration and a wholeness he had not known in his life before. He remembered his childhood dreams, his love of history, the ideals which his Father had instilled in him. And he saw in this place that there were no ranting hypocrites. Just holy men and women putting themselves and their money where their mouths were. Running risks, putting in the time, simply being there. Never throughout that siege did he pray with a priest. Mostly he stayed in his corner. But his conviction grew that he had found his spiritual home.

Of course he had phoned his Father. Of course he had contacted Sue. Of course there had been concern back home. His Father was practically on first name terms with a solicitor in the City, had met him for a cup of coffee when last on business down south. A call to him had ended on an optimistic note. Of course the whole situation soon grew farcical. Within a few days the newspapers and independent radio stations, let alone the international coverage, ensured that. The government's whole response to the "riot" became the question. Embarrassing questions were asked in Parliament. One morning they simply awoke to find the police gone. City-workers began to walk in off the street. Parents and family among them. It was all over. Long before this, those originally arrested had found themselves free. All charges were dropped.

It was as if the whole episode had never happened. The Student returned to his room in res., phoned his family. Nothing much was said, although Father did seem rather happy that for once he had not had to pay out. He and his mates went down the pub. Drank a bit more than usual. But of course none of his mates had been there with him. And he had made no friends among those who had. He drove up to campus the next day. Everything was as it had been. Not even any placards. That Sunday he drove into Town and quietly walked along to the Cathedral and sat quietly in a seat in the back, near the doors.

Back home next vac. the student stayed home on Sunday morning, waited until brekker, and then simply asked Father if he would care to attend church with him. The Church of England. Father's face was still, quiet, a while. He looked thoughtful, then he said "But of course, son". And that was that. They attended regularly together after that, Father and son. Somehow their relationship had become seamless.

Not that the Student changed much outwardly. He still had car crashes that Father had to pay for. He still drank far too much, and wenched as any ex-boarding school boy would when let out on the unsuspecting opposite sex (not in any way compromising his love for Sue, of course). But now he did as his Father had once enjoined him to do. He read the New Testament. And in its pages he found solid foundations for both his political and social views. He never went so far as to be confirmed into his new church. That was far too formal. And anyway would make him stand out. No, he preferred being simply another anonymous worshipper. If nobody asked when he first nervously took Communion alongside his Father, then why should he tell?

During his long discussions about life, the universe, and everything that he had with Chris, they talked about his new-found faith, or beliefs, whatever. Of course it was the value systems of their own western culture that was most dissected. They rejected such obviously illiberal belief systems such as communism, and never really saw the culture of the black African as a menace. To extrapolate from the clan system he had known as a child was simply not on in the Student's minds. They listened to broadcasts by such leaders, couched in western liberal terms, and saw the great groundswell of black opposition in Africa in such a way. They did not understand the dangers of a demagogue working upon the masses and if they attended such rallies they were not able to understand the rhetoric. The values of socialism seemed well-suited to the people that he knew. They did not grasp the attraction of the dictatorship of the proletariat, or of the rule of the many by the few that would integrate itself so easily into tribal and customary life.

As for other cultures beyond those they thought that they knew, they understood nothing. Well able to criticise their own morality and culture, they did not understand the absolutes which were sustained in other cultures such as Islam. Oh, theirs was a generation which toyed with Zen, but mostly as a philosophic rejection of materialism. They understood little. That was to change. And not for the Student. It was Chris who broke away from that which he rejected in his society first.

He and his girlfriend simply left. To begin not the life of wandering hippies, but one in which they would explore their inner selves through living and working in what was for them exotic societies, earning their living through good old-fashioned sale of the skills they possessed; he as a language teacher and communicator, she as a girl able to turn her hand to everything. Southern Europe and South America was where they began, the rhythms of the music and the tempo of life most enticing. They were to find their feet criss-crossing the world, with the exception of North America and Australasia whose societies were so similar to those which they had rejected at home.

Funnily enough, this rootless drifter was to be one of the Student's firmest anchors in life as his own beliefs were battered by life. The two friends communicated by every media available to them, and the constant flow of discussion and argument strengthened them both.

However the Student felt more alone. News of chaos and war from Home intensified each day. Soon he knew he would have to burn his bridges. The letters from Gideon grew more stilted than ever. And finally ceased. His Father's attempts to find out his whereabouts failed. During his last holidays before graduation Father visited Gideon's parents. He was handed one last letter. It stated, simply, that Gideon had left the land of his birth. He would return. But it was best that they talk no more. The time for talking was done. The words on the page blurred.

The student understood. His discussions with Gideon, the closest friend of his childhood, had been put into perspective. He remembered the letters that had become mere recitations of doings. No thoughts at all. The intervals grew longer, the incomprehension greater, until there seemed no point. He realised that he had reserved his real arguments for Chris, Stephan, Sue. They saw things from where he was himself coming from.

The threats inherent in his relationship with Gideon had inadvertently warned him off. He understood, now.

To Gideon, he was a part of his past. Once a friend on very unequal terms. A paternalistic capitalist perhaps. Now an enemy.

He remembered a couple of lines from TS Eliot. He was not sure about the context but it described where he was at. "Home is where one starts from. As we grow older the world becomes stranger, the pattern more complicated."

He burnt the letter. The words were engraved on his heart and their meaning was to change as his life changed. He felt the loss. He felt it deeply. However hard it had been to get through to him in letters, he knew that Gideon was a part of him. As he was of Gideon.

He tried to remember what he had read of Wyrd. How it governed life. Dispassionate. Fate, but the spinning of a life story was not inevitable. Man could still influence his life.

That final term there was little room for grieving. He studied hard, and he lived hard. Be casual, be cool. What's wrong with living? His skin had grown thicker, although his heart was more tender now. Sue took on a greater meaning in his life. But a bloke had to relax from all that study. Frenetic outbursts and birds. There was joy in the music in the night-club and disco; a kind of joy in the life he led drinking cold beers by the cricket grounds and rugger fields that summer and autumn. For he knew that soon he would be going home. His boyhood over and that his choices had been made. Only his graduation remained.

He remembered that morning. To celebrate the big day, he and Rob, his neighbor in res., had decided on their first champagne breakfast, before breakfast. The toasts, the cheers, the toasts and the taunts, as the rising sun took the sharp edges off the mountains in front of them. By the third bottle (well, we bought them and there will never be this day again) the trees on the mountain slopes had blurred as well, and they remembered the long days spent studying for this moment, days in which time had been at a premium, and during which they had discovered one way to release pent-up tension and exercise their bodies. If they both emerged on the long verandah at the same time they would shadow-box, duck and weave, throw controlled punches, all against the shouts of, "Shut up, you selfish bastards!" from other rooms along the verandah.

When one said "remember the old one-two?" they began boxing, crazily. He hit Rob on the ear, slipping the while, and Rob cracked him one on the cheekbone. He gleefully punched Rob in the eye before their fellow students, who had been watching this weird and wonderful celebration, pulled them apart.

"Hey, you idiots are going to kill each other! Are you crazy?" the two grinned, then looked at their clothes, felt the blood trickling down their cheeks.

"Hell, we better get cleaned up. Hell, think of our folks. What the hell will they be thinking?"

Both came from thousands of miles away, and both their families had arrived yesterday for the big event. They were both staying at a fabulous colonial-style hotel on the slopes of the mountain. Both their fathers knew that their wives deserved the treat. Their parents would be dressed up to the nines, and really happy. All four had celebrated together the evening before, when the students had introduced themselves and their friend.

And now the two stars in their folks' lives were in an utter mess. Frantically they tried to repair the damage, cover missing buttons and small tears, clean up some of the blood.

"Hell, how do I cover this up?" asked Rob, looking at his cut ear, still dripping blood. "Sticking plaster will be pretty obvious."

"Ah, shut up, what about my cheek," said the other.

"You'll just have to drive up to the campus holding your hankies tight," chortled a friend. "But what you are going to do about that black eye, Rob..."

"Anybody got sun-glasses," Rob shouted. "I'll only take them off in the Hall. Stand in the shadows... Oh, you Bastard!"

They made it. Drove up, clutching hankies tightly to their battered faces. Rob in his sunglasses.

"Hey, you look cool, man..."

The seating. Listening to the speeches. Pride and achievement.

Then slowly parading up to the capping ceremony. Catching a glimpse of his Mother and Father mid-way down the hall.

Mother, unbelieving, seeing her son with blood trickling down his cheek.

Father - well, he had no time to look again. His name was called. The Vice-Chancellor was waiting for him. And at that moment the flash-bulb popped, capturing his battered features for evermore. And giving him a tale to tell whenever anyone looked at that framed photo on the wall.

Still, the rest of the ceremony passed off smoothly. Thankfully neither of them was walking with difficulty. The panic to clean up had rather sobered them. The pomp and ceremony of his graduation had not really been marred. Mother had never really got around to asking why, and the bleeding had stopped by the time they met up on the steps outside. Oh yes, he remembered his graduation. The end of the interval.

They travelled home together. After the family reunion he knew Sue was waiting for him. At home. There lay his future.

More immediately though, Judy was there, just for him, at the top of the drive up to the house on the hill. She panted up to him as he stepped out from the car. He fondled her graying muzzle, whispered in her ear, kissed the old girl. In old age she almost broke his heart. Ignoring everybody else, Philemon and even his family, he sang "her" song. The old Irish song of longing that was "Oh Danny Boy," with her name interposed. The song he would sing to her one day, he knew, when her time came. She was his childhood and youth, had been his staunchest ally and friend. Had waited for him each term, had always been there for him on his short returns home. Not understanding why he had again to leave, but then always waiting for his return.

Sue was there, waiting in the house. There was only one thing they had to talk through. Should they go or should they stay? Both felt that this was their home. Neither wanted to leave. The price they would have to pay though was his entering the army. The army. The Bush War was hotting up, but both were hopeful. Both hated the idea of the country they loved being run into the ground by terrorists whose political philosophy they suspected was very much one of self-interest. They had read the tales of atrocities and murder. They still hoped for peace. They were certain that if there was a solution, they wanted to be a part of it.

He had no delusions that the paternalistic colonial white system had to go and had to be replaced by one that gave more justice to all. They had seen what had happened in other parts of Africa under majority rule. He had also witnessed the evil that was South African apartheid. There had to be a third way. He was not going to duck out. If it took his being a soldier to give the politicians time to work things out, he would do the time. They made their decision together.

Father looked on. He understood their decision but was not happy with it. But he held his tongue. It was no longer his choice. Oh, he was still able to volunteer his services to the Reserve Forces. But this, now, was no longer his war. Although he listened he said little to influence his son. The Student had now his own choices to make. The Old Liberal's voice was silent.

No-one was listening.

Both were quiet unassuming non-participating Christians. His faith, born in the passionate days of the struggle, had now become a part of him. Perhaps, in truth, it had never really gone away. It informed every aspect of his life. They prayed that their choices be guided by God.

Their faith was very basic to them. He saw everything against the tests of good and bad. So did Sue. In general terms. It strengthened his opinions, but no longer so much in daily life as in politics. Increasingly they both saw the two as separate. The former was becoming as pragmatic a test as the latter. There, Sue was more the matter-of-fact woman. If it hurt nobody that she could see, let it pass. Except for their wedding day, neither went to church much. As often as not the sermon would see him walking out in anger. He would be angry and confused with himself for days thereafter. She had to live with that. Their local church was out for political reasons if nothing else. Neither wanted agro in their lives. They attended the City cathedral once or twice, but it was not important in their lives. Too impersonal.

On the other hand, attending a local congregation could be far too personal. They let it ride. They worshipped together at home. They prayed everywhere together in fact. The world was their church. Like the old celtic church in Britain they saw God in the beauty of their country, and prayed there and then, on the spot.

He thought, chuckling, that much of their love-making was like unto their worship. Something spontaneous, and so very important to them.

They decided to get married immediately after his first call-up and his basic training. He had been in no doubt about the beginnings of his career for some time. History was both his passion and one of his majors at 'varsity – along with Archaeology, English, Political Philosophy, and African government and law. All perfectly reasonable subjects to enter the colony's administration. There was a post within the national archives he had applied for after his Father had seen the advertisement in the government paper. And his army service, when it began, would certainly not hinder his career as a civil servant. Great. He was only slightly surprised to be asked for an interview after only a few days home.

Putting on his only suit he self-consciously made his way into the City where he was welcomed profusely be a large gentleman and a rather buxom blonde lady who pumped his hand and after a short chat containing nothing much else but pleasantries announced he had a job as a junior archivist and would probably receive a letter of confirmation shortly. It was like no job interview he had ever read about and certainly had not been what he was expecting. Rather it seemed as if he was being welcomed into a club which his family had always belonged to.

The down-side was that he had to begin in the capital, and he felt it was asking a bit much after all those years thousands of miles away at university. But, as he found out from his Father, that too was something that could be quickly "sorted". A short delay in commencing his duties was followed by a word in the ear of a few contacts and he was shortly able to receive confirmation that he could begin his duties at his own provincial capital city and thus be able to drive back home every weekend. Sue practically took up residence on the farm and often drove up to the City herself to visit him in the crumbling old residential hotel which was the best his starting salary as a civil servant had been able to secure.

Oh, it was a fairly decent family-run establishment, right across the way from his government offices. They were used to putting up budding young men like him. He soon found himself on very good terms with the black staff, which was especially important since he took most of his meals there as part of a package deal. Speaking their native tongue fluently he was very soon finding his table de hote menu more of a whispered al a carte. He got on especially well with the cook boy and head-waiter, joining them for a fag outside the back of the building in the alley. Of course, the policy on when young gentlemen were expected to be back in their rooms was strict. As was the policy of no young ladies other than family in bedrooms. But with a will, and the cooperation of staff, a way could usually be found to circumvent rules.

The job itself was all he could have wished for. On the first day he was ushered along a musty corridor to the office of his first boss. He was a tall and cadaverous looking academic type, with a pipe firmly clenched in his mouth. He looked ancient. Certainly around forty, but there was a hint of a rogue somewhere in his creased, sun-tanned face.

After a brief introduction, and a few probing questions – certainly more so than had been put his way during his initial interview, he was placed in the capable hands of the office number two, a rather matronly but very well-endowed lady of around thirty. She showed him around.

The building was in that neo-classical style so popular in the twenties. Outside a grand staircase led up to Doric columns fronting the brass-studded double doors. Inside all was brightness and light, an airy atmosphere with the high ceilings so necessary in Africa. Fans whirred away quietly overhead. The public reading room was on this main ground floor, with the "desk" more or less in the middle, situated so that the archivist on duty could oversee most things. Floor to ceiling shelving were filled with books and bound collections. The furniture was of medium oak, lending the right and proper air of gravitas. Overhead, on the first-floor, were the administrative offices. Below ground were the stacks, a maze of rooms filled with arcane documents and books, ever more books. Here a staff of black "boys" laboured to identify and deliver the papers demanded by the public or by the staff.

His duties were divided into two more or less equal halves; helping the public in their search for information and materials, and carrying out his own research programme.

The first was rather fun. Mostly the public wanted help with genealogical research. He soon came to know the tools of the trade. Old colonial records of censuses and land-grants, registers of births, marriages, and deaths, and delving into microfilm and microfiche of English and South African records, and of newspapers and journals.

It was his own personal project that he most enjoyed however. He was given the task of recreating a career. He was taken deep down into the bowels of the building and asked to work up an official biography of a certain colonial secretary, working from scattered official papers and references, newspaper articles, and papers left by contemporaries. First he would try to identify the major sources in the archives, then "gen" up on the period, the life and times of his character. As he began to delve into both the private life of the man and his public life, he began to grow fascinated by his task. He began to grow into a period of which he had not really been aware. The relatively recent past. A forgotten way-station between "real" history and the present. He knew that history could not be cut up into easily digestible chunks, but now he felt that he really understood the flow of time, as he saw decisions made and steps taken that directly influenced him today. There was little romance in the dry tale he was expected to tell, but it became worthwhile. After all, it would be his work that would be used by historians of the period from a variety of different perspectives.

His work might have been seen by some as dry and dusty, but he saw it as truly achieving something. It certainly did not put a dampener on his out-of-hours activities. He made friends among the other young civil servants in his hotel, ranging from accountants to engineers. And together, sometimes with Sue, sometimes without, they enjoyed both the night-life of Town and often drove into the Bush within an hour or two's radius. They swam in dams and lakes, trekked up low hills and picnicked under the shade of thorn trees, sometimes camping out and having an evening barbecue complete with guitar and cheap red wine. That was when he discovered that he had a terrible voice. But following a few beers in the afternoon sun with the atmosphere of a camp-fire and el vino, he was generous with it.

They were never raided by wild animals.

Chapter Ten

The Trooper

"**F**uck this for a game of soldiers!" he panted.

The heat was overpowering, sweat poured down his face, almost blinding him, soaking the band of his camo bush hat... the limp hairs of his armpits and crotch felt full of grinding salt crystals and rind. Still miles to go on this training run, with his full webbing still bouncing, grinding, hurting, his rifle something he almost hated, his boots a torture, his corporal an ogre, his mockery crude and lewd. Then somehow his heart lifted, his boots cleared the ground more easily, as somewhere a chant began and his mates took it up. The corporal grinned back at his colleagues in the jeep behind. His platoon was getting there.

The hymn of hatred to the army's minions finally died out, and the ruthless slog began again. Again the young Trooper closed out the pain, retreated back into his own inner world. He escaped the pain, thought back over the past few months filled with choices and pride and, yes, to all those days of fun spent together.

One day the expected had happened. His call-up arrived. He had to report at barracks to begin his basic training. He went home that weekend and early on Monday morning his parents and Sue drove him down to the barrack gates. Mother was crying, Father rather gruff. Sue began by trying to comfort Mother, then broke down herself. He shook hands with Father and pulled Sue away.

"This is only for basic," he told her. "You know that. This is where they try to turn a bloke like me into a soldier. No way. I am me – you'll see!"

He gave her a big hug and they kissed. He turned and waved to his folks. "Cheers! Be out soon."

The guard at the gate had seen it all before...

He was in that army now. For years the knowledge of it had been weighing him down. He was a reluctant soldier. The embattled colony had taken years to create the forces he was reluctantly about to join.

His society had become almost totally dedicated to war. Every man you met was either a soldier, airman, or reserve policeman. His so-real world had gradually evolved into an unreal one. His normality was to most outside the country abnormal. He remembered his conversations with Stephan.

"It seems such a waste of years of your life," said Stephan. "Fighting to uphold what you don't believe in." This society is so warped by war that it is unreal. People no longer have time for enjoying life."

"Hang about," thought, Stephan. "What of the ancient Greeks. There every citizen too was a soldier. War and being prepared for war was their norm. And what had their societies produced? A king among philosophers who had himself led a fighting retreat from the field of battle? Tragedians who had used their knowledge of the carnage and emotion of war to write moving poetry, from both the vantage point of the victor and of the vanquished. Comedians who, knowing the absurdity of war, brought telling truth to their drama."

"You are a ruddy scientist. Look at Archimedes. These men's genius and creativity was spurred on by war. Dammit, even the earliest history began as accounts of wars fought. It was the

Greek genius that they asked why as well."

"There we go, ruddy historians again," said Stephan. "Well, you would never have got your blessed Hippocrates in a lotus-eating Paradise," said his friend, casually swinging a bolster at his chum's head.

"I think that I know why I made this decision. Why Sue and I made this decision. But don't knock a militarised society as being unreal, old boy. Perhaps it is the stimulation it needs to come up with answers."

"Right on, chum," replied Stephan, "and you always get me when you bring in Sue and quote her as your joint authority. Not much I can say to that, without a punch up the hooter. And mine is too proud a feature to be treated like that!" he grinned.

And now he was in that army. A part of it. Of course he had long thought about the role of the army, and it's place in society, had followed the news, had sketch maps of the country on his wall.

He knew the army had grown out of his society and the war. It was still very much a British force. Its commanders had learnt the hard lessons of the British withdrawal from Empire. In India, Ireland, Cyprus, Malaya, Aden. Each situation different, and the army and its tactics evolving with each new brushfire. Especially they had learnt the lessons of Guerilla warfare well in their long retreat across the Empire.

Malaya had best informed their policy. They had used colonials in that war. Tom would have understood the tactics they were using now.

Isolate the terrorists from the people. Block them getting across the borders or, if that was impossible, locate and destroy them as soon as practicable. Bring overpowering force to bear on any enemy concentrations they discovered. Destroy their communications, supply lines, and disrupt their intelligence. Try

155

to secure the main centres using softly softly policing methods, and above all protect your farmers and businesses, the mainstay of the economy.

To carry out these tasks the combat forces were largely divided into three types, firstly the local national service and reserve units, with black Home Guards, who supported the police. They patrolled in accordance with Intelligence and maintained a presence. They were backed up by the heavy support units, the engineers, medical and signal corps, the artillery, armoured units, the infantry battalions, and Air Force squadrons prepared to support the field troops on campaigns, and which were always prepared for more conventional warfare.

Then there were the regular intelligence units, the scouts who did the recce work, set up OP posts to observe intelligence-derived infiltration and communication routes. These men, both black and white colonials, would even infiltrate suspect villages and terrorist cells. Many would live out alone in the Bush for months at a time. They knew the country as no men before and none would again. They were figures of myth, but also of fear.

Finally there was the regular rapid reaction force. Commando units who were usually chopper born, and would react swiftly to reports of a contact in the Bush. These commandos would also carry out pre-emptive strikes on enemy camps in neighbouring territory. Highly trained and motivated they did become heroes to the folks back home. Especially to the girls, they hoped. Their reputation, unlike the secretive and semi-legendary scouts, spread around the world. In time they attracted so many foreign recruits that their units became almost to resemble the French Foreign Legion.

That was what he, a highly educated and thoughtful bloke, knew of the army and the rest of the organization. Nice and theoretical. A good overview. But he knew he was inside it, looking up and around. It was not a nice perspective. Almost the first thing they had done was to literally attempt, in his eyes, to strip him of his individuality, sanitise him, put him into anonymous fatigues, shave off all his hair so that there was hardly any telling who was who. Until one began looking harder, at the true features of a man. He really began to detest the army but had learnt at boarding school that the only way to survive was to try to stay in the background and blend in. In that respect he became a team player, not picked out in basic training. That, he later understood, was exactly what they wanted.

He tried to explain his feelings and experiences in long letters not only to Sue and Stephan, but to Chris as well. Chris always answered the day he received a letter. Those letters too were important. They did not tell of things that either chap had been up to in the meantime, but spoke of feelings and emotions that arose out of those experiences. But there was not all that much time for letters then.

From the initial medical, through that haircut, to the issue of clothing. The first parade. He found himself switching off. That way the bullshit could not get to him. Not the meticulous inspections which found the tiniest grain of sand on his webbing, loose thread on his blouse, stubble on a fuzzy cheek.

Most of the instructors in basic came from the British Army or the Royal Marines. It was a good life for them. They soon learnt the score.

Unlike the British Army of the time, basic training here was just that. Nobody set out to break that most valuable resource, a white man. Anyway, most people knew someone who knew your family. You were family.

But the uniform. He really hated the kit he was first issued with. A child of the Bush, there was no way he could get on with that crap. In basic they started with the full Korean War layered British uniforms. And WWII jungle webbing. Soon to be discarded and drastically modified in combat. He would always remember those rows of quartermasters dishing the stuff out.

The jokes at the recruits' expense.

Their old British uniform was O.K. in theory, he supposed. The layers of clothing were ideal in that one wore what was required, and the smock and parka were ideal for cold weather or up in the mountains. The multitude of pockets were perfect for long patrol, from the map and first aid pockets on the thigh and knees of the trousers through to those of the smock, with it's internal and external breast pockets, it's side pockets, and the great poacher's pocket inside rear. The other combat layers, such as the parka, middle, etcetera, were never worn. Still, the smock with it's rain-proofing and hood was a useful bit of kit. For now they wore what was prescribed. Once out in the Regiment he would learn that they wore what worked. For now, a T-shirt and shorts were a long way off. This was basic. This was where he learnt discipline, not initiative. He learnt the basics and experience, and his mates would teach him how to be a soldier.

His mates. His draft naturally included faces that he knew; from school, whatever. They were a bunch of blokes who griped together, antagonized each other, played together, and bitched together. That was about it. Mates were people he was yet to meet and make. As English and the Aussies, mates were special. They were there for you, and you there for them. Basic, his basic, was not that sort of world. It was more a time to get through, to bear, until that final hand-shake and "Cheers!"

Finally they gave him his first army-issue rifle. A Lee Enfield .303. Straight out of the box marked with the date-stencil 1953, the year it had so coincidentally returned from Korea and packed away to await some chap like him. He hated that weapon. Forget all the jokes about a bad workman blaming his tools. He KNEW that he was a good shot. But he just could not get that gun to shoot straight.

Despite all the army's attempts, sometimes crude, sometimes lewd, to honour that gun with the title of rifle, he could not do it. Well, not to himself. They finally made him call it such on the parade ground, "This is my rifle, this is my gun; this is for shooting, this is for fun." Crap. It was the bane of his life.

Then the practice began. The drill. The constant inspections. Switch off. Do it their way. Idiots. He did it their way. It became second nature.

The field-work began. Then he shone brightly and briefly until sheer tedium kicked in. The bayonet practice. The life-long humour that began with blood-curdling yells whilst running full-tilt at a hanging sack, the lunge, the step back and retrieval, the charge forward once more. Until they practiced on a prone sack. And his rifle stayed stuck in the sack, and he remained attached to the rifle. Then mathematics came into play. He continued to move forward and described a perfect arc, hitting the dirt hard. Very hard. Dazed, he opened his eyes. Saw a pair of polished boots. He focused, followed those boots upwards, ever upwards, until he saw a sergeant's stripes "Sarge..." he muttered.

"You worthless little Bastard," shouted the sergeant. "Do you see that tree," indicating a bushy piece of greenery on the edge of the training ground.

"Yes, Sergeant!"

"Then do you see that leaf, lower left-hand branch?"

"Yes, Sergeant." What else could he say?

Of course he returned with the wrong leaf. And returned again for the correct one. At a trot. Again. And again.

Shit.

The Inspections, of person, kit, and bed, continued.

All shit.

The drill continued. Parades. The recruits were fucking bullshit. Worse. At least shit had its uses. "Yes, corporal."

Endless physical training accompanied the field-craft. Obstacle courses. Crossing ditches and walls, running over planks, over walls, up ropes. He was fit. That he could handle, as soon his instructors learnt. It was relentless. Then the exercises began at all hours of the night.

Finally the first stage of basic ended. Imperceptibly they began to concentrate more on field-craft and less on PT, more on tactical shake-out and less on drill. First section manoeuvres. Tactical training stressed concealment, camouflage, surprise, taking advantage of success. They were taught to use cover, whether in Bush or Town, how to crawl and snake towards the enemy.

Then came the larger unit cooperation. The theory, lectures, being made to feel a part of a larger whole and to see your place in it. After the conventional infantry warfare theory came section, platoon, company, drills and exercises. Using different weapons. Were taught the outline of fighting in the African Bush in all its forms, whether mountain which plunged down into jungle or the vast grassland punctuated by hills and rivers which shaded into desert. They were taught the basic tactics of outflanking, positioning MG's and snipers, of adapting the tactics to the terrain.

In the final days of training they were shown films of various eventualities and played out the roles, such as a fire-fight in the Bush or being called out in support of the civil authority. Always the same basics however.

It was in these lectures and talks that he realised that most of the regular forces were in fact black, as were much of the Home Guard. This was a multiracial, multicultural organisation. Very much so. White soldiers posted to predominantly black units had to learn the language and customs of those they worked with. And vice versa. In all sorts of specialisations black and white colleagues worked together. If anything the black professionals were more highly disciplined and motivated than their white counterparts. Sometimes white officers attached to the black troops cultivated a paternalistic manner though; often "our lads". He met and chatted to visiting men from such units who visited the camp. He learnt that the legend of the highly efficient mustachioed black sarn't major was for real.

Ferocious, man!

Then, one day, basic was over with a parade of crashing shining boots, a speech, a few words of praise, reading your separate postings, a drink in the bar, a beer.

"Cheers!"

He touched a small copper good luck charm that he had worn throughout basic. His one constant always to hand.

His first battalion was a far more welcoming place. Here his real military training began. There was a general atmosphere of good spirits, of camaraderie. Morale was high. But then this army suffered few defeats. No defeats. No setbacks.

True, as citizen soldiers they were aware of the wider picture. They saw the civilian economy shrink with each attack. They understood the general situation. Somehow, however, in the army world things were very different. Here the male returned to his primordial role. As warriors they knew how good they were, and they were proud. The officers were close to the men. Often they were school friends, or even colleagues at work in the City.

They sat around the camp-fires in high spirits. They shared. He did not. He thought much, said little. Throughout his core beliefs remained untouched. He spoke to his God often, but rarely attended organised army worship. That was not his thing. It provoked too much that was negative.

161

It was in the battalion that they gave him a rifle. A real rifle. A 7.62 SLR to replace that bloody useless .303. and its bloody pull-through. His new friend was to be his friend. He was to take it home with him. It would always be close to hand. He would groom that rifle, talk to it, worry if it played up. The army put a lot into individual marksmanship. And soon, to the surprise of those who had read of his record on the shooting range, he proved himself to be one of the very best shots in the battalion. He could really put all of himself into that one short focused moment before he pulled that trigger.

In most NATO armies the troops are equipped with automatic weapons with light ammunition, two or three times as much as carried by a WWII soldier. They are trained to create an impenetrable zone of fire. Wasting ammo, once a vice, is now a virtue. Only the British Army, the parent army, still trained it's men in sharp-shooting. Not that the infantry section was short of firepower, in jungle warfare you sprayed the Bush, but in the urban environment each man was trained to take out the terrorist whilst leaving the bystander untouched.

In his time with the battalion he was freer to phone Sue and his folks. He wrote less but somehow was able to formulate his thoughts more clearly. Prioritise. Things seemed less jumbled. He saw his path clearer now.

He was issued a Number One Regimental uniform. He had time off. He spent it with Sue, and with the old folks. His first leave came around. After the first hug. The short hair. The moustache. Sue giggling. His Father grunting. Remarks floated out from behind his paper.

Funny how so little was said about the pipe though. The Trooper had a reason for having that pipe. It would really be wrong to say that he had youthful clean-shaven cheeks. It should have been worded as very youthful downy cheeks. A penalty for having started school young and making the first annual call-up, perhaps? Anyhow, there he was. A quiet youngster amongst chaps who fancied themselves men. No matter how much he scraped at those lightly fuzzy cheeks with a razor was he going to see a hair. Nary one.

Somewhere he remembered those grainy old pictures of cheerful youngsters looking just like he did now, and Tom had once upon a time. Photos taken back in the summer of 1940, during the Battle of Britain. Alright, they would not allow a conscript infantryman a black Labrador, but there was surely no regulations against a pipe? So he had bought one from an acquaintance. A real stinkpot, gnarled and black, but now his own.

And that evening when he casually lit up, nobody remarked upon it.

Of course, it was good to be let out, if only for a while. But somehow he wanted to get back in there now; to learn and get his first long period of service behind him.

Back in the battalion his old philosophy still held good. Oh, he had time to drink with the chaps now. He found himself intensely interested in the tactics and methods he was being taught. But still, stay in the background. Blend in. Never stand out.

After joining the Regiment he still had several months to serve before he could go back to civvy life. He was still that small individual cell in the greater body in which he found himself. Now, however, he began to perform that role for which he had been trained.

He found himself performing support duties for the police, manning road-blocks, and carrying out foot patrols in trouble-spots both in Town and country.

Often the roads would be mined. It was easier on the dirt side-roads. Usually it was black civilians that were hurt or killed. No matter. It served the terrorist cause to hamper movement, trade, communication.

Foot patrols in the Bush would go on for several days, sometimes over a week. They would either re-supply at army posts or, if they were instructed to stay well out in the Bush, they might be re-supplied by helicopter. He was rather fortunate in that his section had a couple of teetotallers. He loved teetotallers. Their ration got shared out among the rest – unless that would be stupid in the circs. The same went for non-smokers, of course, but as a pipe-smoker he found one little grumble in life. Cigarette tobacco did not a good pipefull make. By now of course cigarettes were virtually tasteless to him. He found himself packing any odd corner of his kit with baccy.

Patrols were often hearts and mind operations. They would meet people, enter villagers, speak to the elders about any specific concerns, and then report back. Social services and the engineers, or whichever other specialists were required, would follow-up. Often a visit to a village involved advising on security, and of course obtaining intelligence. He began to read people more closely. Observing. Learning how to prompt. Above all they tried to be popular. Chuckling babies were new to him, but he soon caught on. When offered hospitality for the night, as sometimes happened, it was not unknown for soldiers to leave on unexplained walks into the night, nor for village girls to do the same. Little was said, except among the troopers, and it all seemed very much in the spirit of their mission.

Whether mothers and wives would have agreed is another matter. But it was not really the sort of thing that made the evening news. Outside of that particular patrol, of course.

Of course, whilst his side was trying to win hearts and minds, the other side was doing the same. His side could more often provide the medical care the village needed, the access roads, the wells. Often the other side fell back on that well-tried guerilla tactic of terror.

There seemed no limits. Within months he had seen things he could only have read about before, or imagined in his worst nightmares. Headmen beaten, their wives made to kill babies, and raped. No one was exempt from reprisals or terror.

As he and his comrades saw more they grew harder. The soldiers did not try to fight a dirty war. It just happened. It first appeared during chats in barracks or around the campfire. Reports of friendly fire and the shooting of both innocent bystanders and suspected terrs became more commonplace, more acceptable. They were changing as men. Out there they were becoming more trigger-happy too. More and more they began to shoot first and ask questions later. For many of the farm-boys amongst them this was nothing new. They knew there were few rules in the suddenness of the Bush.

A month or two after joining batt he had his first action. It was not planned or intelligence led. It just happened. Some say their first action is a seminal experience. In hindsight, perhaps. It was too sudden. He was too unprepared.

He was taken wholly by surprise. They were advancing along an overgrown path. He was point. He saw a shadowy figure in a clearing. It started as it saw him. Time froze. Then he saw the Kalashnikov lift, the barrel pointing at him. He hit the deck, calling to his mates as he did so.

The corporal passed him, making hand-signals for the patrol to fan out. Then he saw others, figures emerging from the shade where they had been resting, heard the ping of bullets whistling around him, those others wildly firing from the hip, scattering even as the patrol closed around them, opened up.

There were two dead terrs. Pieces of equipment. Those others had been far more surprised and unprepared than the soldiers had been.

He found himself looking down at one of the bodies, lying on it's front, a bullet through his chest. For a moment he feared. Then he knelt and swiftly turned him over. It was not a face he knew. He went over to the other. Again a stranger. He looked around. With an alert defence perimeter, and after radioing in and setting the hounds on the surviving terrs, the men were searching thoroughly for anything that Intelligence might find of use. Searching the dead often turned to looting. Yet they also came up with valuables including watches, wallets, radios, indicating the terrs had recently hit a farmhouse. Yes, they included childrens' toys, even plastic jewellery.

Not much was said as they dragged the bodies and equipment to the landing zone where the chopper was expected. Their patrol was over. The police and intelligence would take over now, assess the evidence, find from whom the stolen goods came. Theirs was to be a quiet evening in the pub.

Few believed him when he told them back home that his first action had been a nothing. Over in moments. Affecting him hardly at all. Yet his Father's eyes understood.

It had affected him. He now knew more of fear. It made him more alert. He remembered how clearly he had seen things in what was almost slow-motion as they had surprised the terrs. He was learning.

As often however a patrol would find itself enjoying the hospitality of a farmer and his family. Often far from help and support, their only link a regular radio update and the news on the wireless, the patrol was very welcome company. Before he would have simply and quietly enjoyed the company, perhaps shyly flirted with a young girl. But now he found himself looking at the children, playing innocently with their toys, wearing their plastic jewellery, and remembering.

At times they would be called out to help the rapid response forces. Again, they would see the horror of civil war, in farmhouse and in village. They would feel fear again. Shoot first into bushes. He began to hate. Seeing his enemy's atrocities made him see the enemy as less than human. Racism began to enter in his veins. Complicated, true. The pity he felt for the raped black girl, overtaken by the lonely lust of the frightened terr far from his world, shading into the sight of the white matron raped many times and then finished by a panga lying in a pool of blood and lying beside her husband in their lounge still holding their rifle. What they did to their own became more of a reason to see them as sub-human. What they did to his kind made him aware of his own skin more than ever before. He was aware of it. He told himself that he was not changing, merely seeing the world differently. But it was his reactions that spoke for him, even if his words remained more considered.

Fear always. Both before setting out and throughout the operation. They would know the joy and relief of having it end. For now.

Then one day Mother wrote. Judy had had to be put to sleep. He had not been able to sing her song to her. Her life that had gone. No song to be sung.

After a while he was offered a stripe. His boyhood in the Bush made him a good bushman, his childhood role as N'kosi to his black peers gave him certain qualities of leadership. He saw it as a gateway to increased privacy. The Trooper became the young lance corporal. One stripe was perfect. No more cleaning the latrines, bugger-all responsibility. Or so he thought then. He would discover than an l/c could be patrol or stick leader way out on a limb. It was true that as he rose he was freer to do his own thing in his own time.

Batt life still included lectures and drill. They would both set ambushes and suffer them in the future. This was mostly a war of small arms. The heavy guns, the armour, was less common than the mortar shell and rocket machine gun, or the rifle, the hand-grenade and the knife. Few would escape for long physically unscathed. He had real confidence in the medical services. Quick. Good. A fast, efficient CasEvac. In fact a junior batt doctor, Edward, was actually a friend of Stephan's from 'varsity. Both men had known of each other through Stephan before they had met. Having an officer as a friend was quite a bonus in the Trooper's life. Edward had his own office cum room, and they could enjoy a quiet drink together. Any "us" and "them" feelings among his comrades faded when he proved himself able to turn the situation to his section's advantage through items he was able to beg, steal, or borrow from the Officers' Mess.

The weirdest thing about the Regiment was the way it was to dominate his life even after his initial stint. Throughout his married life it would be part of their marriage. A sort of social club and sport's club rolled into one. Not that anyone could get him to volunteer for anything other than cricket or horse-riding. Sue spent a lot of her time in the pool though, and chatting to friends.

The Regiment was that, but it was not a family. Everybody knew what it was for. Conversations over the campfire mirrored those in the living-room or lounge. They were the thin red line. Keep the peace. Hold the ring.

Let the politicians have time to work things out.

One evening, driving to barracks, Sue said to him, "This is more fundamental even than apartheid, darling. This is about culture, mores, and what is best for all. Bend those absolutes, my man. Bend."

Those early patrols also in many ways were the best part of the young Trooper's life. He was out there in the midst of some of the most beautiful countryside in the world. He saw the vast bushland, the high mountains, the so-individual rivers and streams, the sunrise and the sunset. He watched the animals, both prêt and predator. On watch he had taught himself to remain fully alert with his sub-conscious mind to danger whilst still being able to fully appreciate all that he saw in the wondrous, wild world around him.

Then his thoughts and imagination would be one. "I crammed in so much that it seems I have lived many lifetimes. And lives. And each eons ago. Now my life quickens. The quick and the dead. Life can be a drill-sergeant, Gideon. Relish the commands. Oh, I love my woman, my dogs, my toys - and wait till you see my toys! Books. Always books. Now time flies. And I know more what you must be thinking. Now I know mortality, but I also know life. Why cannot we share it?"

Out there, amidst all that beauty, all that wonder. Peace was relative. A mother cat would feed her young. Another little one will starve to death because her mother has been killed to provide that meal.

Out there, looking at the colours, hearing the evening sounds, touching the rock, smelling the air, he would worship with both his mind and with his senses.

More often he would not be on guard. He would have enjoyed a smoke after dinner, had a beer or two, and then he would sit staring at the sunset with his arms wrapped around his sunburnt knees, sensing. Those were the times he would not forget.

But the year ends. To hell with it. Back to Sue. Plans and a life to build.

This War is just not cool, man. It's just something we do.

Chapter Eleven

The Man

"**O**h, darling, could you get a couple of pints of milk on your way home?" Sue called.

He was a married man now. Living in a two-bedroomed flat in the City. Gone was the little Anglia. In it's place a black MGB. He had a real job. Real responsibilities. The girl had become the wife.

Now it changes yet again.

His old life was gone. History. Friends had scattered. Stephan had emigrated, with his medical degree to America. His 'varsity friends belonged to another world. Only Chris, who wrote from the oddest of places, kept in touch. With him he was drawn again into the world of philosophy and theorising. The contact was unreal however. Certainly not a part of his daily life. Now the reality, each year, was his army mates. It was his friends from work, from Sue's at the hospital. Their lives apart were diverse, their experiences away from each other very different. But together they were as one and had a devil of a lot more to talk about than most couples.

So long alone in his head. Now he had a friend, always. Not like those friends who had come into his life and drifted out again, each on their own path. Rob, Stephan, even Chris, though their long and tenuous contact allowed him to talk, say things he could to no other. But in many ways it was talking into the void. He was stimulated by Chris's views, but perhaps more by the opportunity of getting what he wanted to say down on paper, to organise his own mind.

He did not include Gideon among those vanished friends. He was a part of him, of his life. Wherever. He spoke of him little.

No. The wife. The friend. Now only the values of his Home, not of abstracts, seemed real. They lived the lives of ordinary young marrieds. They partied a lot, went for drives in "safe" parts of the countryside, though he was becoming more wary wherever they went. The army, his experiences, had done that to him. There was a lot to do in the City.

One thing made their life as a married couple different. He was also a soldier. Subject to call-up. He had not been called out yet, but they both knew it was coming. And it would happen again. And again. They tried to make light of it, but it was always there. Just as many of his army mates were there. In his head.

Oh, most of the male friends of their age were reservists. So the army had to intrude on their lives. Most of his real mates were regulars however. And they would not be coming around. He knew that. And, except for the odd drink in a city bar whilst they were on leave, he stayed away from contacting them, as if by so doing he would be protecting what he had with Sue. Shielding her and them.

The world around them, their world, seemed perfectly normal to him. Chris, even Stephan, began to wonder at his letters, as his world grew increasingly strange to them. He seemed to shy away from anything that shook his reality.

He still read voraciously. The spare bedroom was his study. Very soon they began looking for a little house in the suburbs.

Then the baby happened. A little early but neither had been worrying about preventing pregnancy. Marriage had been the end of all that. They had enjoyed the freedom of sex, anyhow, however, whenever possible. It was Sue who kept coming up with new ways to enjoy his hard young body, and for him to pleasure her sensuous rounded one. He wondered again and again how he could have gotten such a girl. Even in her neat starched uniform she turned him on. Especially then. She delighted him when her shifts allowed her to be home first. Then she would be waiting for him to come home, dressed only in a short loose vest. Then as he ran his hands up her taut body and kissed her she would undress him. Even after a year of marriage they were still like teenagers. They read sexy literature to each other, they watched the most ropy films to pass the censors. They went out together in a crowd, but only saw each other.

He knew that his friends and acquaintances were jealous of him. None of the girls or women he saw in his daily life ever matched up to her. Gad, he loved her. And prove it he would.

So when she told him the good news there was no real surprise. If "it" arrived a little early then it was the plans that had to change, that was all. But they both realised that they did not want their child to have it's first memories to be of the City, or even of suburbia. They would have to get somewhere outside in the countryside. Within commuting range for both of them. All they would need is an old place with a few acres of its own. They could do it up. Hey, maybe even ask their parents for a little labour from the farms? That way they could even get to work with some of their black chums again. Only if they wanted to come and give them a hand, of course.

Of course.

So they began their search. In newspapers, through agents, by driving around the areas they thought best suited. And they found exactly what they were looking for – or at least he knew when she had found exactly the place that she was looking for. She threw her arms around him, tore his clothes off, and made love to him there and then.

"Gosh, lucky there was no agent with us today," he managed to get out, just as she straddled him with her brown legs.

"Oh, that would have been exciting," she said, as she guided him into her and began her vigorous rhythmic movements, her breasts swaying as she moved backwards and forwards, up and down, gradually slowing as he arched up towards her. It was marvelous. Even the baby seemed to gurgle.

The house was old but structurally sound. A low hill cut it off from the urban sprawl. It lay in a shallow valley cut by a lazy old river long ago. It was close enough to the City, they felt, not to be dangerous.

Subconsciously they worked out the racial and security implications in their heads. It was closer to the mainly white suburbs than to the black townships, and the main road north ran nearby, with a couple of hundred yards of dirt track leading to the house. The track ran through arable fields and past a farm-house with all its attendant outbuildings. At one time the house had been owned by the farmer and let out but now he was selling.

He was a tough Dutchman, his wife a sturdy huis-vrou, and they had a hardy looking labour crew. The unspoken agreement underlying the contract was that the two men would look out for each other. Be good neighbours.

The house was in effect an island in the midst of the farmer's fields. All you saw from the property from the track was a wood. It was only as you penetrated up the drive that you saw the old white building. It was cut off by distance and trees from the sporadic traffic noise from the road. There were delightfully old gnarled trees in the front yard, surrounding a large pond which was itself fed from a well, with fruit trees out back. The previous owner had had a vegetable garden and chickens, perhaps even a goat, but they saw a large lawn surrounded by trees and a happy family there, playing on swings, a slide, and outside life revolving around a barbecue. It could be all that they wanted.

Soon. Right now it was dilapidated. It had three bedrooms, a lounge-diner, kitchen, and a wide verandah that ran along all the sides. There were inside connecting doors and a passage and most rooms opened off the kitchen-lounge-dining area but mostly the rooms looked to the outside and to the verandah. It could be their own world screened by trees, an island. With it's own well, septic tank, and out-houses. A garage for two cars. Just right.

Well, after a lot of work, just right. They had both grown up using lavatories in an out-house.

"No ways am I having that here," she said flatly.

"Shit, it'll cost a bomb," he laughed.

"Merde, yourself," she yelled, burrowing into the store-room off the kitchen. "That's out. We are going to have our own little palace here!"

"I knew that continental education would go to your bum," he shouted.

"A palace in the Bush?" He ducked as an old mealie-bag flew straight towards his head. "Okay, okay. I'd settle for making this Happy Valley."

The move itself would be no hassle. A lawyer Father knew could expedite things. They would need a second car, and bought a battered old Landrover.

It certainly was not a seller's market at present, and they could afford the house, even if Sue decided to stop work for a few years.

He was not certain if she would, however. She had a habit of changing her mind, especially if she thought that she knew his. Marriage to her had changed him in a fairly short space of time.

For the first time he was not alone. His friend was with him whenever it counted. And he began to lose some of his anger. His political philosophy was still a guiding force. Now it was more a sense of fairness, and only appeared in his private life, in discussions with friends, and sometimes in his choices. The passion seemed largely spent, although she knew he would occasionally work himself up into a tizzy to prove that he had not really changed. Oh, Sue was her own woman, but she loved him even more whole-heartedly that he could love her. Those years of separation, of trying to say it all in letters or a snatched phone-call. Those brief reunions. For so long she had felt as if the other half of her was missing. It had been.

He had been such a lonely child, separated by so many fundamental differences from even his closest friends. Often these distinctions would be played down in his thoughts. He seemed totally unaware of them. But Gideon had been different. So had Stephan. Even Chris, coming from so topsy turvy a world. Some fundamentals were never touched upon. It was so calming with Sue. They shared so much. So much was unspoken. Did not need to be said. And she deliberately set out to calm him. That, she soon learned, was in her own best interests.

Anyhow, she did not feel quite as he did about politics. Perhaps she felt more, saw more, in real life. It was not going to spoil her life if she could help it. Partly that was because of her job. As a general ward sister she had to divorce herself very often from her work.

She did so, made her life with him very separate. While with him she perhaps transferred all her pent-up feelings to him. She mothered him, and he knew it.

"Hell, let me give you a hand in the kitchen, girl," he'd protest.

"No way. I didn't marry a poofter. This is womans' work."

"Hell. Reverse discrimination, or is this triple?" he'd ask. But she carried on. Had his clothes ready, always had an aspirin to hand if he had over-indulged, had the purges and laxatives to hand after one of his friends' meals – or even after her own mothers.

Not that they went out much. Both preferred their own company. Neither was really a joiner or mixer. Small-talk was rather a hassle at times. Just sitting on your own verandah in your own house was far better in the evenings. For him a pipe and a good spot of history with her reading across from him. The lights flickering somewhat from the generator. Oh, they were happy in that house. They had soon made it livable. With both of them out at work Sue had hired a responsible middle-aged woman to look after the place. Gradually she and Sue were accumulating furniture and wot-not. The basics of course had come from their flat in the City, or been donated by one or other set of parents.

They saw their parents every month or two. His Father seemed to withdraw into himself more and more. Pa rarely listened to the news now. He still thought they, the youngsters, had made the wrong choice in staying and putting down roots. That his son knew. But he never said anything. Sue fussed over him. He liked that. Smiled whenever he saw her.

Mother was still her old self. Still into her clubs, societies, hair-dressers, and loved spending the day with her cronies shopping. And gossiping. She and Sue got on very well but were never close.

He remained rather distant from Sue's own parents, and since she thoroughly enjoyed spending time with Father, they found themselves spending more of their parental weekends with his folks. She was the only one who could get the old reprobate out of his shell nowadays.

His son, however, remained his only friend. The trouble is, their discussions were often stilted now. The Old Boy saw his son's happiness and had no intention of rocking that particular boat.

Often if the couple did take a weekend away, alone, to lodge somewhere on the lakeside, with all mod-cons, he would sit wondering why he had thought this a good idea. Dammit, it was more comfortable at home with his books, with all his historical projects and models. Now that he was a soldier the fighting never went away. Neither of them could enjoy the Bush anymore. They talked about that. About those lone-gone days of innocence that both had spent with their little black peers in the Bush. They talked about a lot. About their choices in life.

At times they saw no answers. Sometimes he would talk passionately and she would sooth.

Resentfully, fed up with justifying, he would shout: "Their leaders were no different from the white capitalists they urge their stupid ignorant followers to fight. They want change. But not for the masses. Only so that they might replace those who made this country, built it. Dammit, the white man had created the very wealth they now want. The pigs want to take over the white mans' trough."

Their trough.

Gideon's trough also?

No, not his. Gideon was an idealist. Was he still? He had grown with the boy. But forget Gideon. Sue was his window on the world.

Mostly they were happy. Their trees did not cut out the outside world but often the two of them did that themselves. They lived quiet peaceful fulfilling lives at home and at work.

Their God was important to them. With both their faith went deep. Not that they attended church much, or mixed overmuch with fellow Christians. They prayed each night together, before the Cross. Their Christian beliefs underpinned their political and social views. They told each other what they would do one day.

How they would like to open a township centre, with Sue handling the medical side, he the adult education. With place to play and read. Games. That sort of thing.

Each day they had to drive to work. A drive that skirted the edge of the townships. At work they saw and worked alongside smartly-dressed black people and those they saw on the City streets seemed nothing out of the ordinary. He knew the other side to their lives, however. He had patrolled the squalid township streets. He knew the degrading poverty they came from. It was a far cry from the happy black children singing in the church on his Father's farm.

If such a paternalistic and kindly a world had shaped Gideon's views, how much more hatred and resentment lurked behind the face of the old cleaner at work?

He knew how he would feel. They wanted to destroy his world and his place in it. He was still a soldier. A reservist defending his way of life and property. How many roads must a man walk down before they call him a man? He began to see a pendulum. It swung and as it grew heavier and swung harder it crushed the swinger.

His was not the world of Bob Dylan. Of southern American civil rights. He was faced with segregation, sure. But equality in his society, he began to see, would not change it. It would sweep it away.

Oh, he still sang "the times they are a-changing", but he began to fear justice. He had to. He still wanted a fairer world. Yet feared what it might bring. As Dylan had sung, it was a funny old world that was coming along. It's dying, but it's hardly been born.

Sue helped him laugh at himself, at his world, as so long ago he had laughed on that train from the south.

He was no longer seeing straight. Life was more complicated than he had ever believed. He did not even know which of his worlds were dying. More and more he knew what he hated, but knew not what he wanted. He remembered his fierce passion at university. But now he saw the logic in the Dutchmen's stance. Apartheid was evil but it was so very logical. His answer, the reason he fought, what he lived for, was a compromise. Can one really fight and die for a compromise? His answer was blowing in the wind.

Oh, the old questioning still reasserts itself. The disgust at hearing a sermon, praying for "our boys in this struggle". Who, he asked himself, is to say which side God is on?

Then the TV news. He felt more and more a pawn in the game.

Conversations with friends reaffirmed his commitment to justice for all. He felt himself always drawn to take a liberal stance. Even against what he knew to be common-sense. Sue watched him, heard him. They had agreed together only the night before that what he was now saying was nonsense. How would the masses be under a black plutocracy who shared only the same skin colour. With few of the white man's cultural inhibitions to restrain them?

But Gideon was not like that, he felt it in his soul. When he did bring his name up, once, she fell quiet.

"But he is only one man," she said. "And one you have not known since boyhood." He never mentioned Gideon to her again.

To friends and colleagues, perhaps, he remained still "The Red". But not to himself. Not to her.

With her old lessons were re-learnt. Old lessons re-taught. The only way to survive was to become more cynical. Believe less. Can one simply say "I don't believe this, boyo..."

He remembered his world of make-believe. The visions in the cave. Of hope in the future through his visions of the past. Of cap and gown. Make your place in the world. Of a benign western elite leading their flock to the promised land. Cynicism is a lesson self-taught.

Life is yours, but only in your own head.

A Father's teaching little understood.

Her time drew closer. They began to talk baby and baby things. Decorate the room, buy toys. Or rather, their two mothers did that.

Towards the end both spent every other weekend in the house with them. He even got to know Sue's father a little better. All he had to do was to listen and not answer. Something that had seemed impossible so short a while ago. This was his world. He had this stage to play upon.

At work there were definite hints that he would soon be promoted. He felt that he had grown into the job but was able to contribute more.

Contribute. An odd word. But this was the play in which he had been cast.

Theirs was a play, however, from which there was no escape. They never did see that happy family playing on that lawn in the dappled sunlight filtering through the leaves... Their baby was never to see daylight at all.

The fighting in the Bush intensified. But theirs was not to be a war tragedy. Their life was to end in a way that is common in almost every large city. The ending of their story would never make the headlines. He would not be found with an empty rifle lying over her body in a pool of blood, surrounded by a dozen dead rebels.

No. She went shopping. She was mugged. The baby lost. Her spine is damaged, her brain. She sank into a coma. She does not know him. Death hung in the air. The damage is irreparable. He held her hand. For an age. He stared at her lovely face. His face. He talked to her. He kissed her. Many times in that timeless world.

For him there was no time. No other voice but his own. He was alone in that room. He pictured her sprawled on the ground that first time they had met. She had jumped up then, full of life. No fussing. Not his Sue. Not then.

He saw not God. He heard him not.

He watched her die. Nodded. Signed the forms. Her heartbeat stopped. Like that. At the touch of a man's finger. He did not think much. His feelings went too deep for that. He simply loved. Unthinkingly. She was his life.

He went back to the house. The empty house. He asked the maid to leave. Surrounded by a tangle of undergrowth, her car with flat tyres and a flatter battery.

He drank. Not to forget. To survive.

He tried so speak to his God. Silence.

He did not curse. He knew now that there was no point.

He was alone.

Roaming the place, he cried out. There was nothing.

His whole being called out. For the companion who had guided his footsteps whom he had never known.

The priest came around. Was told to leave. If the master had gone, what use the acolyte?

Yet he still wore a small copper good luck charm.

He visited no-one. Their parents had flocked to the hospital, of course. But were not welcome after. Father did not approve but he kept Mother away. Sue's parents were simply told to go away.

Only Father got near him. He was the only one who did not talk. With his son he had never had to. They understood each other. Had done from the moment they had heard of Tom's death. Father was Tom to him.

Once he awoke, and in those moments before fully awaking to the horror that was his life he thought he saw Gideon, gazing at him sadly. Like a Byzantine icon. Then he knew, again, that Sue was not there. She had not only been his friend. She was his life.

He never visualised Gideon again.

His Father heard him crying.

His Father's hand did not try to steer him from the bottle. But it did preserve his life.

Not for a new life. For death.

Death was in his soul, in his mind. Death was all around. Life was a nightmare. He slept. He awoke again, and drank. Before he died he had to see to another's death.

He attended the trial. Only Father by his side. Heard the defending council say how deprived this little black boy's life was. How he had come to the City, was homeless, joined his local underground cadre to survive, was known to the police.

How he had sought to steal to secure his place in his new life. He had been driven to theft by his poverty and plight.

He had taken by force what he wanted. However. The means to his end.

That little black bastard had taken his life. The Bastards took. He had always looked for reasons. Now it was so simple.

The sentence came. He felt it not.

He stood outside the Central Prison on the day. Watched the flag lowered. Saw a door in the gate open. Read the note that was pinned there.

He felt empty looking at it. This was not enough.

He left. He looked at them. Seeing not people, only them.

He looked at each passing black differently now. Each seemed a threat. The poor in their poverty. The wealthy in their smug confidence that one day they will lead the cattle. And graze their herds on his land.

He heard not his Father's words. He was there. What was between them would always be there. But he no longer heard. He heard not his friends. Not Stephan. Not Chris. Not now. Talking was shit.

At their house the silence was all. She was not there. Her things all around did nothing, brought him nothing. Death was in him. He had that.

He did not analyse much. Think of God, Fate, or Wyrd. It was not a redeeming death that he sought. He sought nothing. It was merely the working out of his life.

Wyrd. Perhaps there had always been a certain relentless logic in his life. He had always been involved. Even as a child he had wanted to understand the workings of his peoples. He had tried to live in two worlds. He had been taught certain principles in which he had always believed. Call them social justice, call it fair play.

The blatant injustices of apartheid had turned him into an agitator for political reform. He had faced the consequences of such reform in his own land. In his own life. There was no compromise in his life. To try was to destroy.

Chris and Stephan had been wise. They had left for lands in which they would never feel a part of their host society enough to ever allow it to really affect them. They had been there. They had "seen the Elephant", as an American would say. They had known fundamental struggles involving race, religion, freedom and dignity. Never again would they find themselves in such a crucible. To them most other political struggles would seem superficial. Oh, they would still take a stance, form their own opinions on the questions of the day, but never again feel such passion.

Sue and he had tried to live what they had believed were normal, decent, lives. But in an abnormal society they had not been allowed to do so. Her killers had not known her opinions. They simply took her life. Had taken his. There was something else that he knew deep within himself. He hated.

The hatred built. Taking his own life was pointless. He had to play out the game. They had taken her. They would pay. He could take a lot of the bastards with her before he went.

There was no redemption for him. Killing brings no redemption. He no longer had anything to prove or justify.

They wanted him.

Fuck the cunts. They could take him.

He would go to them.

Chapter Twelve

The Commando

He joined the regular army. The one life he had truly despised. The impersonal legionnaire, not the citizen hoplite or old English warrior defending his own. He voluntarily submitted himself to a life of taking orders, of losing his individuality. He did not think such thoughts now. He knew only that this was to be his way. A means to an end.

He chose to join the commandos. He joined a foreign legion. Elite soldiers and fearsome warriors. Their exploits made the news around the world. On international newsreels they either swaggered across the screen in smart regimentals or patrolled the vast Bushveld in short shorts, T-shirts, and cut-down kit. They were soldiers, parachutists, swimmers, used both for rapid response counter-insurgency and incursions into foreign lands where their masters sent them to hunt out the beasts in their lairs.

When, long, long, ago he first saw two commandos strolling across his old parade ground dressed in a casual mixture of uniform from World War II through Korea, Vietnam, and Malaya, he had asked who those buggers were. They had told him, in no uncertain terms. He had admired their ability to retain their individuality in this damned army. That he really liked. Yet they were professional, and his life had no room in it for that type of man. He was just a foot-soldier who admired their casual behaviour and lack of formal discipline from afar. Now he joined them.

His selection interview posed no problems. To the board he came across as a quietly spoken young man, determined and purposeful. His record was good He passed the very tough selection course itself with flying colours. Soon he was wearing the badge of his unit. Girls looked twice at him in the street, or when he sat alone at a table. His good looks went well with his reticence. The uniform that he wore spoke to them of the glamorous deeds they saw being carried out by men like himself on television, in the news, or in the glossy magazines.

The young blokes in the bar who wanted to buy him a round, those women who had looked at him twice; all were rebuffed. Oh so very politely.

He gave little of his private self to his new comrades. Only enough for them to recognise that he could be trusted. He would be there for them. Dammit, as he grimly reminded himself, if he did not look after them they would not be able to kill the terr bastards efficiently. After a while fewer questions were asked. He was not disliked. He was respected. Even came to be regarded as "lucky". You stood a better chance with him.

He was left alone off-duty. His commitment and obvious determination impressed his superiors. He was to gain rank in the days to come. With rank came added responsibility for others. Even concern for their private troubles and joys. That he handled as if at one remove. "A sympathetic robot" said one trooper of his boss.

His detachment was in itself a source of strength. Friendship or otherwise did not influence his judgement of his comrades. He saw both their strengths and their weaknesses for the task in hand. He was a good soldier, and he was a good leader. Often his individualism saved his superiors from their own folly. Much of his achievement in the Bush was due to the boyhood skills learnt with Gideon and his other black chums. He was a bushman as much at home in the mountains, in jungle valleys, or out on the broad veld.

"Lucky" he was.

He made for a lousy companion. Made no friends as such, although in the course of things he grew close to a few men in his immediate stick. His leave he spent alone, seeking oblivion, Sometimes he shared his off-duty time with those other members of his unit who were hard-bitten bachelors. But he put rather a dampener on things. He had no small-talk, had no interest in women. He did not talk of sex, of sport, or even of politics. He rarely smiled. He was shit company.

An occasional visit home saw him staying away from his old haunts. Once he clambered up to his cave. It had returned to the past. There were few signs that he had been there. He had joined the traces of the past. He sat at the entrance and looked out over the river and plain. He saw no shapes in the heat-haze, or in the distant mountains. He felt no ghosts. Nothing.

He could not blame his God. He knew that evil happened, and, if he thought about it, knew that it was how the individual coped or tried to cope with the consequences was what counted. If he thought about it he might have thought of his soul being itself in mortal peril. If he did.

He did not give a shit. It was empty out there.

His Mother's love frustrated him. He caused much pain, and although faintly aware of it he did nothing to ease it. With his Father he was also distant. There seemed so little to say. Perhaps the truth was that Father understood all too well, and that deep pain in Father's eyes said it all.

He read few letters from past friends since her death. He never answered his old 'varsity chum Chris. What was there to philosophise about, or to understand? Why ask "why?"

"When" was the only question over which one had any control. Sometimes, anyway.

Stephan too was someone in the past. In him were embodied too many memories. Father told him that he had telephoned once or twice.

The men in his troop were a diverse lot. Most were Africans like himself, but he found himself closer to the outsiders. Men who talked not of home, but lived in the here and now.

They were part of a true Foreign Legion. British ex-regulars who joined up again for a stint in Africa had their own varied reasons, as did the many French, Germans, Italians, and other Europeans. The Old Dominions made up a large proportion of battle-hardened vets. Aussies, Kiwis, Canucks. Many of the South Africans felt that they would rather stop the enemy here, in the land of The English Rooinek, before he reached their own country. Many were American ex-Vietnam vets, men who craved excitement, men who believed that they were simply continuing the fight that had only ended a few years before. The same was true of the Aussies. But their reasons were hard to classify. Each individual soldier had his own reasons. Only by knowing the man could one tell his motives. Maybe. These men were not mercenaries in the usual sense. They served exactly as did their British and Colonial counterparts, for the same meager pay, and under the same Spartan conditions. Whatever their reasons, they were not in it for the money.

He understood Vietnam veterans like Aussie Geoff and Chuck, an American, blokes he fought with, and often drank with, who were veterans of a lost war. Like him, they fought for themselves. Unlike him, they still enjoyed the lives they risked so carelessly. They drank and caroused. Sought out the chicks, wore their unit badges boldly as they swaggered down a street.

These two were the core of his fighting unit. Others came and went. Aussie Geoff from the big City and Chuck from some small one-horse town in the featureless farmlands of Middle America.

They became close through a relationship of trust. They knew each would look out for the other in the Bush. Even in the bar. The other two would talk, sometimes, of their lives. Of the good and the bad. He would listen. Usually that was enough.

Geoff was a cocky bastard, a Flash Harry on leave, wearing his cocked slouch hat at a jaunty angle. A regular favourite with the birds. He could talk the hind leg of a donkey, could Geoff. The life and soul of the party if he wanted to be. Lean and lanky he could contort his limbs into almost any shape. Yet darkly handsome. With long lantern jawed features. A ladies' man, sure. A party man too. But he rarely received mail, and there was that something in his eyes that discouraged personal probing.

He would usually begin the evening with the boys. Later on, if he saw his mate in the corner nursing his drink he would come over. Then after a few more he would begin to talk quietly. Or sometimes he would just swagger over, doff his cap, and demand that he be bought another before disappearing off into the night. He could rouse a chuckle many times. But even Geoff failed to make the other's eyes laugh.

Chuck too was long and lean. Fair and chiseled. He would drink with the lads, but quietly, and never seemed to get drunk. No-one in that small society knew what he really got up to on his time off. He too would see his mate drinking quietly in a dark corner and would often join him. Sometimes they would talk shop. Sometimes simply share each other's company. He was a man of few words. They heard a few Vietnam anecdotes, and knew enough of the man in action to believe them all to be true. He was a truly skilled survivalist. He taught the Commando much in the time they spent together. The two men watched each other's backs. Owed their lives to each other's reactions and to each other's skill in bushcraft. So often that there would be no talk of such things between them.

Not that the three of them spent most of their time together alone in bars much. Life was too uncertain and too filled with attractions for the other two to spend their valuable off-duty hours with an old fart. No. The time they spent together was mostly in the Bush. When the situation had to be analysed. Before or after action, when the other two found their mate's coolness and matter-of-fact words just what they needed.

The unit he had joined was known throughout the military world as one of the best at its job. That job was multifaceted. They were primarily airborne assault troops. Helicopter borne. They were also parachutists. Their instructors were usually ex-British Paras. Not difficult, that part of his training, after his first glimpse of the earth thousands of feet below from a Dak. He learnt how to exit the aircraft, how to guide the webs, to land and roll.

He felt little fear of the canopy never opening though.

He absorbed it all. He became what he wanted to be. What in essence he already was.

The selection course was just the beginning of his training. To him everything he was involved in, surrounded by, became just another tool for the job. Both men and equipment. His job began.

He learnt wherever, however. He learnt much from Chuck, beginning with his kit. Every man in the unit modified his equipment. Chuck had had his own more comfortable, lighter, and more capacious webbing sorted. Of course the Bush soldier's vital companions were the knife, a good machete for bush-whacking, cutting shelter-poles, firewood, etc, a 7" knife with saw-blade for cutting light wood, and his canteen, usually with a metal cap or cup for boiling.

Then came the rest. Webbing stuffed with ammo, spare mags for the MG, grenades, radio. His personal survival kit would include water purification tablets, durable, high nutrition food (choc bars),waterproof matches, a mirror for signaling, and fire-lighting, a poncho as tent and groundsheet, which he also used for shade, cammo, and used to catch rainwater. Then those little essentials. A nylon string, two large bandanas (slings, bandages, water strainers), fishing hooks, a multi-purpose Swiss Army knife, small torch, and of course a compact first aid kit.

Their clothing was drastically cut down, often to shorts, T-shirt, veldt-shoes. Only the webbing and equipment remained complete. Weapons were camouflaged. The combat cap with its multifarious folding curtains and flaps was soon cut down. The ubiquitous leather Bush hat for some, a baseball cap for others, like Chuck. Layered kit was useful if on long patrol out in the Bush, but not for chopper-borne troops. Their kit was left very much up to the individual. Yet was frequently checked by the NCO's. Woe betide a man who omitted anything thought vital. One got to know the few rules. And stuck by them. It was your life on the line. And that of your mates.

It was that camaraderie, that mateship, that kept them going, that helped them make it almost every time.

Even on leave their regulation uniform felt weird. Yet somehow when they appeared on the rare parade they turned out as the smartest soldiers in the army. For them such occasions were not routine but special. Their chance to show the world who they were, in their smart blues.

His life became an extraordinary mix of comfortable station life and the very real horrors of the battlefield. The transition took place within a half-hour.

Contact would often be made by intelligence-led recce, Scouts, through informers, or through reports by civilians. Once an area was located, ground troops would be sent in as stops. Then the air-assault would go in. Then light helicopters would disgorge sticks of four men including a MAG gunner, the number of sticks depending on the size of the enemy groups. Sometimes a couple of sticks, sometimes a troop of thirty men, rarely an entire squadron, all covered by a helicopter gun-ship cruising overhead with its 20mm cannon, and possibly a fixed wing aircraft with rocket pods, bombs, and napalm. Scarcity of choppers meant reinforcement by plane, each carrying five sticks of paratroopers.

First the air-strike would soften up the target, then the troopers would sweep in, driving towards the centre of the target, driving the terrs into an ever decreasing area or forcing them to disperse onto the waiting guns of the stop forces.

It was murderous work. Slow, cautious work. Sometimes the enemy would panic, run, surrender. More often than not they would fight desperately, set up hasty ambush points, fighting with the terrain. The air would be thick with bullets, some aimed, some fired off wildly. The wounded terr with a grenade clutched to his belly. The fake surrender. The routine shooting again and again of "dead" bodies. The close quarter no-holds barred fighting. Knife and bayonet work. Rifle butts and pangas.

Only in that brief moment after a successful contact, when the area had been scouted, the recce done, the intelligence gathered, did they see him... relax. He counted the kill himself. But afterwards, for a brief moment when the corpses were dragged together and were being examined, he would tense as he looked at their faces. Then he would, yes, relax.

A contact rarely lasted much beyond a few hours. Then back to base. A smoke. A beer. And each to his own.

He still saw something of what was inside of him. He knew. Just was not bothered by what he saw.

His every word and action seemed to the point. After a while his comrades felt that they knew where they stood with him. Time was important to him. He would rarely tarry or dally. He took few chances. That made for a bad soldier, endangered others. He was a good soldier, a good leader. His men believed that they could trust him, as did his superiors. And he WAS "Lucky".

Out would come the battered old pipe, the baccy from wherever it had been secreted about his person, and he would seem, for a brief while, open. As if something had just flown in front of the moon and taken something of himself into the night with it.

He remembered the fighter boys of the Battle of Britain.

It produced strains so immense that they must crack if not relieved.

He refused relief. He no longer took his leave allowance. He spent his time alone on the range, or with a glass in the bar. Then Chuck or Geoff would join him. They had been through a lot together. They did not talk much. Other times Chuck would wander off making for a merry group with plans to go somewhere else. It seemed to make not much odds. It was not in alcohol that he found oblivion, but in his job. And he became very good at it.

Months passed. Years. The Commando was part of the scene. Men relied on his mere presence. The siren would sound. They leapt up, dropped what they had been doing, thinking. Grabbed kit long inspected. Sergeant shouting when he saw items missing. Good man. Heard the rotors turn, motors throb. Scrambled aboard. Swooped away. Damn. Crouched there. Or swung the MG in lazy arcs under watchful eyes. Orders shouted. Voices, wind, noise, sweat.

The chopper pilots stayed low over the trees, searching out a landing zone, move in, and as quickly the troopers are out. With his rifle levelled, moving fast, crouched, to cover his mates behind. Peering. Arm waving, moving in. Shots striking around him. He fires. The MG lays down a lead carpet to their front. Grenades. Shrieks. They move on, firing from the hip. He stumbles over a dead body. More ahead. The airman had caught the terrs in thin cover. He heard shots in the distance. Slowly the units converged. It was over. No-one hurt. They gathered the gooks. Their bodies sprawled and dangled every which way.

They checked the area. Posted sentries. An occasional shot in the distance. They did not look up. They smoked. His old pipe. It was over for now.

Sometimes men collected souvenirs. O.K. He drew the line at the gold teeth and body-parts. He knew what he was fighting. Men, just like himself. That was why he hated the fucking bastards . Others saw the butchery the cunts had carried out on farmers, travellers, villagers. The mutilation, the savagery, and that took away their compunction. They saw them as munts, kaffirs, black bastards, commies. No way. That was racism. He saw them as men. Men who had choice.

Other men would rather shoot the fuckers. Not him. He took as many prisoners as he could. They would talk, Special Branch would see to that. Then others would suffer. Be caught. Then the sentence. Would die. The slow death by hanging. No, that was not enough, it had not been enough then, was not now. But it was better than a quick bullet. The bastards.

Sometimes they had an overnight action. Sometimes they would spend many days out in the Bush in a camp surrounded by a ring of claymore mines, wired to the sentry in the middle of the circle. If attacked he would fire them all, blowing the attackers to Kingdom come.

On such nights, with the sentry posted, with only the familiar sounds of the Bush, Chuck would talk, softly. At such times both Geoff and the Commando listened.They learnt of another life, of a childhood that he had only read tidbits of, and of a war lost and gone to all but those who had fought in it.

Geoff would tell them of surfing and yachting in the bay, those long-legged Aussie beauties. But neither of them talked much of their families. They were still fighting a war. Especially Chuck. He was a mean bastard to those who did not know him. Until they saw him with a wounded animal. By the roadside as much as in the Bush. He loved animals. Everything, it seemed, except creepy-crawlies and snakes and other bloody reptiles.

"They wuz born frum an egg, not knowing their Mama. They got no feelings Ah kin relate to. No ways," he said.

He would always be bringing in some creature which was hurt or sick, and nurse it back with single-mindedness and plain cussedness. He even built little pens out back. His Alsatian bitch quite gave up on doing much about it. Geoff swore she helped as nurse and playmate, her tongue cleaning up a small deer or even a terrified kitten. His acquaintances around their various posts came to regard his constant requests for re-housing a dog or cat as routine. As did the local villages.

In fact he did spend a lot of his time among the local village's animals, applying a lifetime of experience and a heart full of sympathy. A tough bugger, sure.

In those quiet evenings the hard man spoke softly, wistfully, around the campfire. Not only of 'Nam lost but of returning to a society who just wanted to forget the boys they had sent out there. Those vets had not lost the war, they knew that. Yet there was no way they were heroes back home. Graphic photographs of Vietnamese casualties of war, of a naked little Vietnamese girl, reports of massacres at some place called My Lai or wherever. It rubbed off on all of them. They resented it. They resented the smugness, the ignorance. They were out of the loop. Their experiences made them different. They felt increasingly out of touch, treated as pariahs. Most would try and live with it. A few, like Chuck, would search out another war against the same enemy. Not because he was a hard unfeeling brute, but because they had made it impossible for him to do anything else. Even then his wry humour had seen him through. He had turned to a bigger world. He had chosen a way of life. For now. Not for ever. He had something to work out of him before he could settle. He was saving. There would be that little place. With a girl. In his home country, if not in his old home Town. Not there. Not now, not yet.

At such times, hearing his friend, the Commando's mind would wander. Begin to engage. Once he had thought about his country's future. When a settlement was reached, would his country be a land his people could be a part of? Then a shade would come down over his eyes. He would almost blink. Shit. All shit. He carefully placed another couple of dry branches on the fire. Now his country was already dead. There was one day that it and his whole world had died. Sue.

But Chuck talked. He listened. Then Geoff would lighten the tone. Out would come one of his jokes from some inexhaustible store. Chuck would try to match him, the two of them would end up stifling their laughter and aiming mock punches at each other.

For Geoff too it was not now. He could hardly imagine any such set-up. Ever. For him the fucking road would wind on, and on. Life was a game, sure enough, and he was going to play it. Like his geet. That guitar was either something that the blokes loved back in barracks – or loathed. Because along with the strings came a rather unusual voice.

They both came from worlds so different from anything the Commando had personally experienced. In detail. But all three friends shared one thing. All had been brought up in lands where they had learnt about nature, it's beauty and it's power. The Outback or the Tennessee mountains. The details were different. The animals and plants were different. But the harsh realities of a world that any bastard who had spent his life in a city never knew and could never understand were always present. They could adapt to his Bush. They had tricks to learn but they knew what they were at. Here both Geoff and Chuck found him their mentor. He talked little of himself but a lot about the Bush. The other two learnt things from him that they could not have learnt from an instructor at base or even from books. They listened as he told them about tracking, about spoor, about how to avoid danger from plant and animal. He told them more about the land, of the tell-tale signs left by a man in the Bush. He told them of the tracker, of the tracker's people. He introduced them to him in the tracker's own language. Often he would sit with them at their fire, although somewhat apart. On the trail, if there was time, he would point out things to them.

Of all the others beside his two mates, it was the yellow-brown tracker in his floppy hat and baggy shirt that he most understood. Deceptively scrawny legs poking out of his shorts. He was barefoot. Could run on almost any surface, however hot, thorny, or rocky. The man's motives were as clear to him as were those of the other veterans. There would be the same shares of belief in a cause, greed, and simple enjoyment of a way of life. And deep down, if he were a little yellow man, he knew that he would feel the race-hatred in his blood. The Commando remembered their sign in his cave. The little men were so much a part of him, of his mind and his soul. They had never given up. First they had struggled against the black warriors, their stone against the black man's iron spears and arrowheads, and then with the harshest regions on earth to which they had been driven by the blacks. The hate directed at those arrogant black farmers and ranchers who had moved in and taken his land, had played with his women, had almost exterminated his people, had driven them from the fertile plains into the harsh desert fringes. They were men of stone fighting men of iron.

To the blacks, and to many of the much later whites, his people were not fully human. If they were hungry they killed a cow. To the black tribesman his cattle were everything. "His" cattle. The Khoi San had no idea of private property, of land owned or cattle herded. A war of annihilation followed, over decades, centuries, all the way from the equator down to the last barren wastes into which his people had been driven. He remembered the stories he had learnt. He remembered their presence in his boyhood retreat. Their art was everywhere in his Africa, loudly proclaiming that this land had been theirs. Their art was delicate, the colours defying the passing of time, seeming to reach out and capture the spirit of the animals they portrayed. Their art was a lament.

The Khoi San were not animals. They had adapted both physically and mentally to their land of exile. They were the most expert hunters and trackers in all Africa. Now they had the white man's iron. Forged and crafted with beautiful skill to kill the black man. Oh yes. He could understand the tracker fondling his gun at the outer edge of the campfire.

He saw many things. Things that angered the others. Frustrated them. Made them hate. The carnage was not all one sided. He saw villages after they had called in the hunters and canberras. The dead. The dying. Feeling nothing. The baby sucking at his dead Mother's teats.

Then one day Geoff was blown to smithereens.

Chuck had seen the wounded gook. Had held back on the trigger. Not this one. He looked only a boy. Saw the gook move his hand.

The Commando had seen Chuck's forbearance out of the corner of his eye. He saw. When the grenade killed Geoff he learnt that he could still feel. He had believed that he had no-one. Not now. His being there had been so important, yet his life had been so fragile. There had been no last dying words. No lingering death. It just took an instant. Standing over his mutilated friend in the Bush. Geoff. A lifeless torn corpse. He felt unreal. The Bush that his friend had known still seemed the same. He looked up at the blue bowl of African sky. It was the same as that which his friend had looked at a few minutes before. And then there were two. He and Chuck.

He looked at Chuck. It was all over. No more to be done. The American looked sick. He began to tremble. His legs felt weak, his belly was empty but he heaved.

Take no prisoners. Just shoot. Hack. They were still.

Back at camp he and Chuck sat alone. His comrades let them be.

Their invincibility had gone. His mind was blank. He felt old. His finger twitched. He stared at it. Saw it. It was a part of his body. It was still part of a living, working, machine. A machine. That was all he was.

As he sat staring into the fire he remembered The Man. His probable hopes. And here they were. A life fucked up by people and their hierarchies that you never could get away from once you left the farm, could you?

"Sorry, Father. I had it all worked out at 'varsity, didn't I?"

Then he thought of her. He saw no image in his mind. She was not a part of this life.

"Still, thank God I have one certainty. I'll be home soon, Darling. There will be that one last op..."

Time ground on. He killed efficiently, led his men well. With no other distractions, he was very good at what he did.

There were no Samaritans who tried to save his soul, cheer him up, take him out of himself, or who would try to save him from himself. Most people simply accepted him on his own terms, and got on with their own lives.

He was promoted. Now he saw the intelligence reports on which his attacks were based. He read the scores. Scoreboards almost. Of terrorists killed, of Security Forces casualties. The reports on the terrorist leaders. He read even of Gideon in the terse reports of Special Branch.

When he had left he had made contact with the guerillas. His education and quick intelligence had marked him out from the very first. He had made enemies. He had been sent to study in Russia. Had continued his Law studies. Even there, a foreign cold hard land where he and his kind bonded, he had made few if any friends. He had not taken the usual path of one as highly educated as he. A lawyer could expect to become an administrator, a leader, even a propagandist. As a spokesman for the cause his precise English and clever legal brain would be invaluable.

Intelligence could not explain why he had chosen the path that he had and stayed as a field commander. Yet as such he was a dangerous threat. He had earned himself some ill-deserved notoriety. He had few rivals as a bush fighter.

He remained a loner. He had not even a woman. Rather he had many women. Gideon's journey had been long. He had become a dangerous man. There seemed no prospect of his rising in the party hierarchy. He was not that sort of man. He was a soldier, doing the politicians' work for them.

Are we not both that, asked the Commando? He read the summary reports, the analysis, again. He shook his head tiredly. The kaffir bastard, he thought unemotionally.

Would he remember?

So who gave a shit?

The anger, the hatred, the killing rage, burned lower now. It was still within him. But he was tired. He had seen too much. He had done too much. Now he fought the terrorist bastards grimly. Sleep and food were only bodily functions. They prepared him for the work he had to do. He had become a regular soldier in order to carry out one task and in that he was still deadly efficient.

There was dope as an alternative to booze. Never in the Bush. He never saw it then, never smelt it. On base, at night, it helped him. There was no hangover the next day.

The time came when day after day they would hear the tannoy blare. Occasionally three contacts a day. Morning, noon, and night. The faces changed, the units changed, as men, unwounded, unhurt, but simply deathly tired, fell out. Combat fatigue was a phrase. The reality was deathly tiredness. Everything was looser. Everything was the same. The old guard was there. Always Chuck and his stick of gum. His caustic comments came from his inscrutable Cherokee face. Some days the first call would be early. Contact. NCO's and officers met for a hasty briefing. The mechanics completed their final maintenance checks on the choppers. Men ate a quick breakfast, stuffing ready-made sandwiches and small flasks into any available pocket or pouch, then sat outside on the grass, checking their weapons. A last smoke.

The call through the tannoy. Like their fathers in the Battle of Britain they rushed to their aircraft. Like them they felt this to be the climax of their war.

Then for a few days there was a break in sightings. The men gathered around their huts and smoked. A few wondered. Most were so exhausted they simply accepted the fact and slept. Others went drinking and carousing down at the local, under strict curfew. It seemed a lull before a storm.

Then came indications that a big op. was being mounted.

There were reports from the Scouts that a large company, perhaps 300, maybe more, had crossed the river. This was a big one. They had to be hit hard, destroyed, before they could disperse. The whole unit was going in, immediately after the Air Force. Stops would be sent out early. The Scouts had them under observation, would flank them. Then track any survivors who escaped the aeroplanes, the fire-force , the stops. Wipe them out. This was a big one.

He felt no anticipation. The past few weeks had exhausted even him. These weeks had changed even him. The purpose was still there, but the purpose of an automaton. He functioned. He did his job. Something that had long driven him had gone. Had left him. He no longer fought to kill. He just fought. Sue was still there in his dreams and in his every waking moment, but he saw her differently now. As a goal in herself. She seemed to reach out to him. Only in her arms could he find anything again. My God. My God!

His cause had turned him into a ruthless killer, an expert soldier. Had helped him to forge one of the best teams in the unit. Now he was changing. Weary. Empty.

Chuck saw it. Tried to shake him out of it. Instead the American began to hear memories that he had never shared before. Chuck heard names he had not heard of before. He heard him tell it not as an act of cleansing, but as a monologue without hope, without fear. The tone of the monologue Chuck heard was dead. There was no emphasis. One incident was told as flatly as the next. His Father, Sue, Gideon. All were part of his whole. Yet not as living people. Dead. All dead. The names were words. He did not talk for long. From after the evening meal until the sun finally went down. That was all.

The next day they heard of the op. Talking stopped when the orders came through. The routine of preparation took over. After all, this was just another op., however big the staff believed it to be. The same checks had to be made, briefings gone through.

A lot of the blokes hoped that this one might really count for something. Perhaps something like this might break the enemy's back.

Others knew how many more were out there. However many bases the Scouts and S.A.S. took out along the borders, there always seemed more. No, for them this was just another job.

That night he could not telephone his Father. Blanket security had been imposed. He missed that, tonight. He would have liked to hear his voice.

"For one last time..." he almost found himself adding. Oh Shit. His Father. Pa. Tom. He had remembered. He had thought about them. Something had stirred within him. It was not love. It was certainly not hate.

He did not pray that night. He could not. There was nothing to say to Him. He had nothing to say to Him. He stared at the starry sky, open-eyed. Things came back to him. Not memories, exactly. Just things.

He thought of the op. Gideon flickered, and was gone. A fresh-faced handsome youth, eager and quick.

"The quick and the dead," he whispered.

"If Gideon were there...?"

"Have they cupped their hands to drink?" he asked himself, his thoughts drifting with exhaustion.

Then he slept. He saw Sue's arms reach out toward him.

Chapter Thirteen

The Other

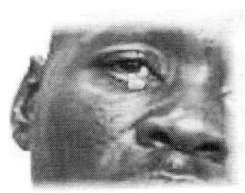

Gideon was there.

He led them, a man who had proved his worth in many clashes with the security forces. His face was scarred and hard-set. His body a whiplash. Ever since crossing the border he and his men had been like coiled springs. His equipment, and theirs, was pared down to the bare essentials. He was the chosen leader of the largest infiltration for a very long time. His mission to score a massive propaganda coup, at whatever cost. They were expendable. He knew that.

Unlike other commanders he had never been trapped. Oft thwarted, occasionally defeated, he brought his boys back. Unlike so many others. Men heard of only again in the security forces' bulletins. His methods were his own. He was respected by the tribespeople whose land his missions traversed. He controlled his commissars. He fought his own war. He was too useful to his masters to question. He had been saved for this day. As had his men.

Not to start a final conflagration. His mission was to light a beacon for the oppressed. He knew that. His fighters knew that. Some had been soldiers in the oppressor's army. Many had friends and relatives still fighting for them. In this civil war the enemy was not anonymous.

The enemy. My brothers.

The guerillas had no logistics back-up, bar having a guide who knew the area. In uninhabited areas they had no re-supply.

Gideon's story was but one story among the 300 stories that had gathered together for this attack. Every man there had his own reasons, his own individual loves and fears.

They knew that they would most likely all be killed. If they succeeded, the army would hunt the surviving fighters like dogs. They would commit every resource they had to wiping them out. They had been chosen because they were veterans. His veterans; brave, resourceful, determined. They were on low rations now, Gideon had taken them by the long route, the safest route. He knew these men, what they were capable of. They still had enough. They still joshed each other, joked before sleep. Their clothes were torn but their weapons were clean and well-oiled.

Gideon's purpose was to inflict damage not on isolated farm houses or security posts, nor on scattered villages, but to hit the security forces hard in a supposedly cleared area, before splitting up, each group then acting independently under it's own leaders. That was the plan.

First the Battle.

The numerically small white society could not take what he was attempting to do. The people knew that. No amount of propaganda on their side could ease the pain. There would be too many telegrams, too many suffering families for that. Their success would be counted in enemy dead, not in the cost to themselves. More men would follow in these dead comrades' footsteps. Their propaganda machine would see to that.

Gideon's face gave little of his thoughts away. He had never been by nature a hard man. But survival in the struggle he fought had changed him utterly. Not even the Political Commissars knew his thoughts. He held himself aloof. They did not know him, but they knew of him. His story remained his own. And this night whatever he thought alone in his hollow scratched in the dirt, only he knew.

He thought of his Home. He believed that his father still worked well with the man, the farmer. He thought of his old friend, his master. He imagined life as it was there. Or, rather, as it had been. He had had little contact with his family. A few letters smuggled through in the early days. Then nothing. He hoped that the War had been kind to them all, that no fighting had taken place near the farm. He had heard nothing, and he studied the news broadcast by the enemy when he had time.

He had heard of the attack that had killed his friend's wife Sue. He had felt that deeply. He wished that...

No, it was stupid to think that. It was just as stupid as wanting to contact his old friend. Not his master now. Just a man caught up in something terrible, but something that had to happen. This war was inevitable. It was the only way. He knew the Boy he had known had to have died long ago, changed into a different sort of man, just as he had. Gideon also knew that he had to be a part of the white man's Security Forces. There was no point in dwelling on that, however.

There was not much point in thinking of the past either. If he could ever return to that farm everything would be different. He would have won. A man would be judged by what he had made of himself, not by the colour of his skin. But he was unlikely to return to either the farm or to his family.

He remembered the constant minor humiliations of his youth. Oh, as a boy he had lived in what seemed the normal world. But as a youth he had moved among others. Known feelings that his white friend and master could never understand despite their long conversations. As he grew and learnt more, Gideon had had to join in the struggle. To stand aside was not an option.

The patterns of individual thinking that he had developed in the Bush did not stand him in good stead in Moscow or with the party leadership. His faith in the law had gone long before he had left to join the comrades. He had seen too many injustices in the courts, too much legislation had been passed for him to be able to work under that colonial law. The fundamental rights of the individual which he and his white friend had discussed late at night were fatally undermined. The basic code he believed in, the core of English law, was denied to him. He could never be a black Englishman now. Certainly not a black English lawyer. All that would be left to him would be to try and find those nooks and crannies and loopholes his oppressors had overlooked. He would be a shyster, a dog worrying at the rubbish, looking for something worthwhile at the bottom of the heap.

No ways. Right. He had learnt of the law codes of continental Europe and especially of Russia. He had seen how even the most outwardly enlightened system lent itself to abuse by the ruling elite and could so easily be used to stifle dissent, to oppress the people.

He saw the leaders of his own party revelling in their new authority. He saw life in Russia – as much as he was allowed to see – and knew that was not what he wanted to be a part of. He looked at his leaders' flash cars, their lavish lifestyle, and during conversation he learnt of their absolute ignorance of their own people, of their needs, wants, desires. Not that any other of the opposition parties were any different. Something had died within him as he listened to those ambitious, ruthless, men, and as he heard their plans. He had asked to cut short his legal studies and returned to his military training.

As a fighter and a leader of men he excelled. No longer did he discuss, argue, make enemies in high places with his awkward questions and high principles. He could have risen high in the councils of the opposition. He could not. They had become politicians. He became a single-minded fighter. His leaders knew something of this. They were not stupid men. Gideon remained apart. A different animal. A top commander, privy to the most confidential operational planning, but not part of the party's inner circle. He was reserved for all the most risky missions. He had pulled most of those missions off. Everything he did was vital to the cause. His leaders knew that. They also knew that they did not much want him around after the victory of the people.

He was the ideal man to lead this mission. He stood a chance of succeeding where few others could. Yet he was definitely expendable.

His rank and position in the party allowed him the privacy he needed. He rarely socialised. He enjoyed a few of the perks of his position. Yet lived a life devoid of any of the luxuries his peers took by now for granted. It was as if every night spent at base was simply a rest by a stream before his next mission. He was a man and had never slept with the same woman for two successive nights.

This night would probably be his last. It had come to this. He knew that if he fell he alone would one day have a martyr's statue erected in a city square somewhere. He alone. No such commemoration for his men. They would die unsung. A number in his enemies' statistics. Their deaths glossed over in the party propaganda. His normally expressionless mouth twitched. Equality came down to this.

For all of those men this was a night when, despite the presence of their comrades about them, they were each very much alone. Some reached out by word or touch, to their friends, but found little comfort there. If they were able to they could only find some inner peace within themselves or from their own individual experiences and history.

Many wore some token, some charm, from a loved one on campaign, and held them close this night.

Gideon wore an old pewter cross. Tonight he held it to his chest.

He stared up at the stars shining in the clear African sky. His Africa. Their Africa. No words came. Thoughts flickered and died.

A comrade shook him awake two hours before dawn.

The contact had been made. The choppers would come. The Scouts were out there. Watching. This time they did not flee into the Bush. He sought out where they would hover and disembark their deadly cargo. He had chosen this killing-ground long ago. Now he, Gideon, was here. He meant to hit them before they could hit him. With what for his men was overwhelming firepower. They would kill many. Fight a battle that would echo around the entire world. Kill their young men. Hurt their fathers.

He gathered his tired hungry rag-tailed men and positioned them. They prepared their positions. He had every man check his weapons. They waited. Men in tattered jungle green. Men tired. Men scared. Men who prayed, those who merely believed. Men determined.

Here endeth the first lesson...

Finale

The Commando crouched by the door of the Chopper, swinging the MG in an arc over the thick thorn-scrub Bush below him. The other three men in his stick were tensed to jump. He almost involuntarily touched a small copper good luck charm. He heard, saw, the jets scream in. The rockets taking out and softening up their target.

Waiting. The old sailor's prayer dinning in his brain; "Lord For What we are about to receive make us truly thankful."

"Go Go GO!"

He jumped.

Gideon.

The cough of Kalashnikovs.

"MY GOD!"

About the Author

Geoffrey Storey grew up in the Africa of the 60's and 70's. A historian, he lives in Lincolnshire with his wife Penelope and his two dogs. He enjoys driving, boating, shooting, and the English countryside. He travels widely to historic sites and to get the feel of his subject. Above all he loves a pint of real ale and his pipe whilst engaged in reading and research.